"Whew! A curl-your-toes, hot and sweaty erotic romance! I did not put this book down until I read it cover to cover. . . . I highly recommend this one." —*Fresh Fiction*

"*Twin Fantasies* is every woman's fantasy!"

—Bertrice Small, *New York Times* bestselling author

MORE ACCLAIM FOR THE NOVELS OF OPAL CAREW

"Wonderfully written . . . I highly recommend this tale."

—*Romance Reviews Today*

"An amazing, intoxicating love story . . . Definitely an author to keep your eye on." —*Romance Junkies*

"An outstanding novel . . . I encourage you to read this exceptional book." —*The Road to Romance*

"This book is extremely HOT! Ms. Carew had me squirming in my seat while reading this story. This book was so great I want to read more stories by this author."

—*Coffee Time Romance*

SIX

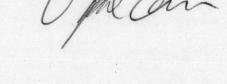

OPAL CAREW

St. Martin's Griffin
New York

This is a work of fiction. All of the characters, organizations, and events portrayed in this novel are either products of the author's imagination or are used fictitiously.

SIX. Copyright © 2008 by Elizabeth Batten-Carew. All rights reserved. Printed in the United States of America. For information, address St. Martin's Press, 175 Fifth Avenue, New York, N.Y. 10010.

www.stmartins.com

Library of Congress Cataloging-in-Publication Data

Carew, Opal.
    Six / Opal Carew.—1st ed.
        p.   cm.
    ISBN-13: 978-0-312-38479-1
    ISBN-10: 0-312-38479-3
    1. Resorts—Fiction.   2. Group sex—Fiction.   I. Title.
PR9199.4.C367S59   2009
813'.6—dc22

                                                            2008030154

First Edition: January 2009

10   9   8   7   6   5   4   3   2   1

To Jason,

*Whose strength of will
and sheer determination
I admire.
Paired with your
compassion and intelligence,
you are an unstoppable force.*

*Thank you for being
a part of my world.*

ACKNOWLEDGMENTS

As always, Mark, Matt, and Jason, you are the best and I love you always.

Colette, your continued support means a lot to me. Rose, you are the best editor I could hope for, and I appreciate all you do for me. Emily, I wouldn't be here without you. Thanks to all of you.

SIX

ONE

Harmony stared at the glossy pamphlet again, with the photos of vivid blue, tropical water, white sandy beaches, and lovely villas along the water. Aiden would be here in a few minutes and then . . .

She leaned back in her chair and frowned. Was she going to tell him or would she continue to keep it a secret from him—just like she had everyone else over the past twelve years?

Her heart clenched and she drummed her fingertips on the brochure. For the first time in her life, she felt she had met a man she might have a future with—and she didn't want to endanger that. But the time had come for her to make a decision.

At the rat-a-tat-tat of small pellets hitting her apartment window, she glanced at the view beyond the glass. Not that there was anything to see but swirls of snow. The eerie sound of the winter wind sent shivers through her. She glanced at the pamphlet again, laid out on the dark-stained cherry desk in her living room. Stroking her finger along the palm trees bathed in golden sunlight, she imagined the sun warming her bikini-clad body and fine sand pushing between her toes as she walked barefoot along the beach. The rhythmic sound of the surf washing along the shore drew her further into the lovely world of tropical heat and no worries as she left the cold, wintry world of Buffalo, New York, behind her.

The doorbell rang and Harmony folded up the pamphlet, stuck it in her desk drawer, and stood up.

She crossed to the fireplace and flicked the switch to start the fire—she loved having a gas fireplace—then padded across the plush blue carpet, her bare toes sinking into the pile. She pulled open the door.

"Hi, sweetheart." Aiden's cinnamon brown eyes glowed with warmth as he smiled at her, revealing a charming dimple in his cheek and softening the strong line of his square jaw. She wanted to run her fingers through the dark brown waves of his wind-tousled hair, still aglitter with big, fat snowflakes. He stomped his boots to knock off the snow clinging to them and handed her his burgundy jacket.

"Come here." He grinned as he grabbed her and pulled her into his arms.

His nose and cheeks were red and his skin was cold to the touch as his lips met hers hungrily. His arms came around her and her nipples hardened as his cold body pressed against her warm one. Finally, their lips parted and his gaze met hers.

"I've missed you," he said.

She smiled and drew back, taking his hand and leading him into the living room.

"It's only been two days." And he'd called her yesterday. He was the most attentive boyfriend she'd ever had . . . and she loved it.

His arm hooked around her waist and he nuzzled her ear.

"Two days too long as far as I'm concerned."

He walked with her to the couch and sat down beside her. They snuggled together in front of the warm fire.

"Hot chocolate?" she asked.

He nodded and she lifted the stainless steel carafe from the tray on the coffee table and poured them both a mug. The sweet smell of chocolate filled the air. She'd prepared a batch before he arrived, knowing he'd appreciate a cup to help him warm up after his drive here through the blizzard.

She really enjoyed Aiden's company. They had met almost a year ago on a local ski trip to Kissing Bridge Ski Area in Glenwood—actually two weeks after she'd returned from her annual vacation. Leena, one of her friends from work, had talked her into going and, a total novice, Harmony had gone down the hill too fast and fallen, her legs twisted and her skis crossed in an awkward jumble.

Aiden Curtis had whooshed to a stop in an impressive

spray of powder and helped her to her feet. No small task given that her skis kept sliding out from under her. Somehow, he'd managed to get her vertical again and safely down the hill. He'd spent the afternoon coaching her and soon had her going down the hill in a somewhat competent manner, if not with grace and speed.

Now they'd been together almost a year, and she couldn't go away on vacation without telling him about—

"You seem deep in thought. Anything you want to share?"

"No, I . . . uh, was just thinking about work and . . . I'm going to be taking a week off soon—to go on vacation."

"Oh?" He smiled and tightened his arm around her shoulders, drawing her closer to the warmth of his body. "Do you want to go somewhere together?"

She stiffened a little. "Actually, I've already made plans with friends."

"Really? You haven't mentioned anything about it."

"I know. I've been meaning to tell you . . ."

The timer went off in the kitchen and she sucked in a breath.

"Oh, that's the lasagna," she said. "I'll go toss the salad and put the garlic bread in the oven. How about you grab a bottle of wine?"

She would tell him after dinner.

As they ate, Aiden talked about his new project. He'd been asked to design a building for a big company developing a campus on the outskirts of the city. It was a huge project for him and they wanted something impressive and different—something that would make a statement. Aiden was very concerned about creating environmentally friendly buildings and that was a major reason they'd selected him—and one of the things she loved about him. They wanted to let the community know they were environmentally aware and intended to promote green practices.

Harmony loved how he was concerned with more than just getting a job done. He had principles and he stuck by them. He wanted to make the world a better place in any way he could.

They cleared the table and filled the dishwasher together, then sat down on the couch with the bottle of wine and soft music playing in the background. Aiden topped off her glass.

"Honey, I know you wanted to tell me something about your vacation, but could we wait until a little later for that? There's something I wanted to ask you."

"Sure." She welcomed the chance to put it off for a while longer. She relaxed into the couch.

"You know, we've been going out for close to a year now."

She smiled and nodded. "Our anniversary is in four weeks."

She leaned toward him with a smile and rested her hand on his chest, enjoying the feel of solid muscle beneath her fingers. Gazing into his earnest brown eyes, she wanted to fall into his arms and ravage him. To explore his muscular, masculine body in detail. His broad, well-defined shoulders, the sexy planes of his chest, his six-pack abs.

A sharp yearning clutched at her insides. Her hand slid down his chest and over his tight stomach. She wanted to do things to him she'd never done to him before. Sexy, naughty things.

She drew in a deep breath. But she wouldn't.

He grasped her wandering hand as it headed lower still, and held it between his.

"Sweetheart, if you keep doing that, I won't be able to keep my hands off you long enough to finish this."

She leaned in and nuzzled his neck, delighted that she had such a strong effect on him.

She couldn't believe she'd actually held off for almost a month before making love to him when they'd first started dating.

She'd been afraid that having sex with him would open a Pandora's box of desires and that she would do something . . . inappropriate. She didn't want to see that look of disgust on Aiden's face, the same one she'd seen before.

She'd been afraid of losing him. As much as she loved sex—and she really did love sex—after that incident with Lance . . . Her stomach knotted. It had left her shaken and extremely gun-shy.

Of course, as she'd gotten to know and trust Aiden, she'd realized he would never treat her that way. When she finally began an intimate relationship with him, though, she'd promised herself to keep things . . . restrained. Missionary position, minimal talking, nothing out of the ordinary. Vanilla all the way!

Aiden stood up in front of her and sank to one knee. He kissed her hand, his lips brushing gently against her knuckles, sending tingles up her arm as he gazed deeply into her eyes.

"Harmony, I love you."

The air locked in her lungs as she realized what he was going to do.

"I want to spend my life with you."

Oh, God, this wasn't happening.

"Will you marry me?"

Aiden felt her hand turn cold as shock permeated her features.

Damn. He had hoped she would throw herself into his arms and shout yes at the top of her lungs, then kiss him passionately . . . then start tearing off his clothes and . . .

But at the look of her now, he didn't know if she would give him a chance after all. Had he blown it? If she turned down his proposal, would she end it between them?

There weren't a lot of relationships that could survive a rejection like that. An image of Mia's face flashed through his mind, and his jaw clenched tighter. Hopefully, his relationship with Harmony wouldn't have to.

"So, sweetheart, what do you say?"

"I . . . uh . . ."

She shook her head and gazed down at their joined hands. His heart sank.

"Are you saying no?"

"Oh, no," she said as she stroked his cheek.

"You don't look very happy for a woman who's accepting a proposal of marriage."

"I know, I . . ." She shook her head, clearly searching for words.

"Do you love me?" he asked.

She gazed straight into his eyes and drew in a deep breath. A decision was clicking away in that brain of hers. After what felt like a lifetime, she nodded.

"I do." She drew in a deep breath. "I really do."

His mouth widened in a smile. "But?"

She exhaled. "But, I'd like to hold off answering you."

His gut clenched in pain. If Harmony truly loved him, why would she need to wait?

"For how long?"

"I . . ." She rested her hand on his cheek again. "Oh, Aiden, I know it's a lot to ask, but could you be patient a little longer? I have something I need to tell you . . . something about me . . . and I'm not sure you'll still want to ask me that question once you know."

That sounded ominous, but he knew in his heart there was nothing she could say to dissuade him from wanting to marry her. He took her hand again.

"Harmony, I've already asked. Now what do you want to tell me?"

She shook her head. "I don't want to tell you. Not yet."

She cupped his face between her hands. "Before you decide you don't want me—"

"That'll never happen," he said as he drew her hand to his mouth and kissed her palm. "You can tell me anything and I won't change my mind."

"Then, can you wait? I'll tell you later . . . tomorrow . . ." Her eyes glittered in the firelight. "Because, right now . . ." She stroked his face, curling her fingers around his cheek, then gliding them along his whisker-roughened jaw. "I want to make love."

TWO

Aiden grinned. "I'm certainly not going to refuse an offer like that."

As much as he wanted her answer, it was clear she needed reassurance . . . and if making love would give her that, he was happy to oblige.

She smiled and squeezed his hand.

"Wait here." She stood up and walked across the room, then disappeared into the bedroom.

He sipped his wine, wondering what secret Harmony wanted to tell him. What could be so awful that she'd consider it a threat to their relationship?

Moments later, he heard the bedroom door open and turned his head. His breath locked in his lungs at the sight of Harmony standing in the doorway, looking like every man's dream of a sex goddess. The loose-flowing black silk wrap she wore was a perfect match for her glossy black hair, which flowed over her shoulders. Sheer black stockings hugged her long legs from toe to thigh, held up by black garters.

"Harmony, you look . . ." He just shook his head, unable to find the words. Usually, she wore a simple satin nightgown in white or a pastel shade, which was sexy in a demure way, but a far cry from this sexy, purposefully *arousing* outfit. . . . His cock hardened.

"You like it?" she asked as she stepped forward.

His gaze didn't stray from her long, sexy legs . . . until she flung open the black wrap she wore to reveal a black lace bra that pushed her breasts up and out in a delightful swell of white flesh. Her nipples pushed at the edge of the lace, barely contained. She swirled around in a full circle, the fluid black silk an elegant halo around her, then she turned away from him and leaned over, as if to pick something up from the floor. Her round behind was naked except for a tiny triangle of lace at the top of her black thong. As she leaned down, she stroked her hand over the delightful curve of her derriere, sending ripples of need through him.

He wanted to grab her, throw her down on the floor, and ravage her right there.

She stepped forward, then knelt in front of him.

"You mean so much to me." Her fingers tangled around his belt buckle and she released it, tugged down his zipper, then stroked the length of his cock still confined in the cotton of his boxers.

"Harmony, that—"

She slipped inside his boxers and he felt her touch on his

naked cock. The rate of his pulse soared like a rocket. She drew his throbbing erection from his pants, then wrapped her hand around it and pumped a couple of times, sending desire shooting through him.

"Honey, let me . . ." He wanted to kiss her, to hold her, to please her, but she leaned forward and kissed the tip of his cock, then her lips surrounded him and she sucked him into her mouth.

Harmony loved the feel of Aiden's cock in her mouth. It was thick and hard. She stroked with her hands as her tongue trailed around the edge of the corona. His labored breathing encouraged her and she sucked him deep into her mouth. She cupped his balls as she sucked and pulsed on his delicious cock.

His hands clung to her head. She sucked and pumped, swirled her lips around the head, then sucked him deep again.

"Oh . . . sweetheart, I'm going to . . . ah . . ."

She sucked harder, squeezing him in her mouth, then quickly pulled away. She stroked her hands around his cheeks and kissed him.

"Take off your pants."

His eyes lit with excitement at her words. He stood up and dropped his pants to the floor, then sat down again. She smiled, then slid onto his lap, her knees on either side of him so he was sandwiched between her naked thighs. She kissed him again, sliding her tongue between his lips and caressing his mouth. His tongue stroked under hers and tangled in an enthusiastic dance.

She pushed herself to her knees, then glided her damp slit along his cock. It twitched beneath her.

She reached around behind her and unfastened her bra, then slipped the straps off her shoulders. She smiled at him and peeled the bra from her body, revealing her naked breasts.

"Beautiful." His masculine hands cupped her breasts, sweetly and reverently. Her nipples budded, straining against his palms.

She murmured in his ear. "I love you touching them. Now take them in your mouth."

He leaned forward and sucked one nipple into his hot mouth. Fire blazed from the tip of her nipple down through her crotch and she undulated forward again, stroking his cock with her wet slit.

Her body stroked him, again and again, as his mouth ravished her breasts. He sucked and she moaned, pivoting her pelvis forward and back.

"Harmony, you're driving me crazy." He wrapped his arms around her and lifted, then eased her onto the couch. He knelt beside her supine body and kissed her breasts, suckling the nipples, licking the aureoles, then kissing down her stomach while he warmed her breasts in his hands, still squeezing and stroking them.

He hooked his fingers under the elastic of her thong, then eased it down and off. Her lacy garter belt and stockings framed her naked pussy. His cock twitched at the sight. She lay fully exposed in front of him and basked in the heat of his gaze, which trailed from breast to crotch and back, then shifted to her face.

He kissed her mouth, then his gaze returned to her black pubic curls. He stroked a finger over them, then slid along her slit. He sucked in a breath when he felt how wet she was. He leaned forward then she felt his mouth cover her as he kissed between her legs. His fingers slid inside her and she arched forward.

His tongue found her clit as his fingers pulsed inside her. An incredible heat built within her and she wanted his long, hard cock inside her.

Pleasure built in an overwhelming barrage of heat. She grabbed a handful of his shirt and pulled him upward.

"Aiden . . ."

She tugged harder.

He glanced at her. "What is it, love?"

"Come here. Kiss me."

He obliged then shifted to return to her pussy.

"No." She grasped his cock and pumped. "Kiss me again."

He groaned, then met her lips with fiery passion.

"I want you to fuck me," she said. "Drive your cock into me so hard I'll feel it into next week."

His eyes widened in shock at her words.

She'd always held herself back while making love with Aiden, not wanting him to think her too wanton, but now she needed to give him a taste of what she was really like in bed, without the restraints she usually kept on her language and behavior.

But was she scaring him away?

He kissed her, driving her anxiety away, replacing it with unadulterated lust.

She widened her legs.

"Fuck me, baby," she implored. "I want you deep inside me."

He rocked his pelvis forward and his cock thrust into her in a searing lance of pleasure.

"Oh, yes." She wrapped her legs around him, giving him deeper access.

He thrust and thrust again.

"Yes, sweetheart." She clung to him, riding the wave of passion. "Give it to me. Hard. Fast."

Aiden couldn't believe the words coming from his sweet Harmony. And he loved it.

He thrust into her again and again, loving the feel of her silky, hot flesh surrounding him. Stroking him.

His balls tensed and his cock swelled. He felt the heat of his semen coursing through him and releasing into her body.

She wailed as he groaned. A heavenly bliss surrounded him as they shared an incredible orgasm. He kept thrusting as she moaned in ecstasy.

Finally, he slowed as she relaxed into his arms. He rolled onto his side and drew her tight against him. She rested her head on his shoulder and he luxuriated in the deep, soothing sound of her breathing. He'd never felt so good with anyone before, and he wondered why she had hidden her delightfully sexy side.

Harmony opened her eyes to the smell of bacon and fresh-brewed coffee. Aiden stood beside the bed holding a tray with a covered plate and a steaming cup of coffee. He set the tray on her bedside table and sat down beside her.

"Good morning." He leaned in and kissed her. His lips tasted of coffee and sugar.

She licked his lips and smiled. He looked absolutely delicious shirtless in his dark gray boxers. The combination of his broad-shouldered, lean muscled body with his dynamite smile made her insides quiver. She ran her fingers down his chest, then over the ripples of his abs as she nuzzled his neck. She dipped her tongue into the hollow of his collar bone, dabbing at the salty skin, then her cheek brushed against the hard muscles of his chest as she glided downward. She lapped her tongue over his small, hard nipples. When she ventured lower, he grabbed her hand and kissed it, drawing her upward.

"Breakfast . . . then I'll let you have your way with me again."

She smiled and pushed herself to a sitting position. He tucked another pillow behind her, then placed the tray over her lap. He removed the shiny cover from the plate, revealing scrambled eggs with melted cheese and several strips of bacon. A small basket on the side contained a croissant and a little bowl of strawberry jam. She sipped the coffee, which already had the cream and sugar added.

She spread jam on the croissant. "Breakfast in bed. Well, I'm a lucky girl."

"Hmm. Almost as lucky as I am."

He stretched out on the bed beside her, his elbow bent, his head propped on his hand, and watched her eat. When she finished the last tasty mouthful and sighed, he took the tray away. By the time she'd showered and dressed, he'd already finished the dishes.

"You know, I could get used to this." She sat on a stool at the eating area of the kitchen counter. He leaned in and kissed her.

"That's exactly what I'm banking on. If you'll recall, I did ask you to marry me last night." He sat down beside her. "Now, do you want to tell me what it was you wouldn't tell me last night? The thing you thought would put me off marrying you."

Oh, damn. Her jaw tightened. The time had finally come.

Her gaze fell to the counter and rested on her intertwined hands. She nodded, then sucked in a deep breath.

"Every year since university, I've gone away on a vacation with a group of friends."

This story hadn't started the way Aiden had expected. Not that he really knew what he had expected. But the fact she went on vacation with friends didn't seem so bad.

"These are friends I met in university." She glanced from her hands to his face. "Well, I guess you figured that out."

"So you go on vacation with these people. You want to continue doing so? Is that it? Because we can certainly arrange to—"

She raised her hand. "No. I mean, yes, I'd like to keep doing it . . . well, I'm not sure anymore . . . I've been thinking a lot about it this year and reevaluating . . ." She shook her head. "I'm sorry, this is just . . . hard."

He took her hands in his. "It doesn't have to be. Whatever it is, we'll work it out."

"The point is, we go away every year . . . and have for the past twelve years . . . the six of us, and we . . . have fun."

He nodded.

"A *lot* of fun."

"That's great."

She sighed and got up to pace the kitchen floor.

"You're really not getting this. There are three women and three men . . ."

At her pause, then her exasperated expression, his brow furrowed.

"Do you think I'll be jealous because some of your friends are guys?" He would have thought she knew him better than that. "Do you have history with one of these men? Is that what you're worried about?"

She nodded. "You could say that. Not just history."

"You've been intimate with one of them?"

"No."

He sighed in relief. He wouldn't like the idea of her going away on vacation with a man she'd had sex with, even though he knew he wouldn't stand in the way if that's what she wanted to do. After all, the past was the past.

"I've been intimate with all of them."

His gaze locked with hers. It took a moment for the words to sink in.

"All of them?"

She hesitated, as though choosing her words carefully.

"The other women have been intimate with all of them, too."

He cleared his throat. "So this is . . . a kind of lovers' reunion?"

"In a way."

Sure, maybe they'd been a group of friends in university and wound up dating each other at different times. Of course, they'd all become close and now they met once a year to rehash old times.

"I understand. After all, it's all innocent, right?"

She pursed her lips. "No, not so innocent. We actually meet for a full week of no-holds-barred sex."

He chuckled, but her grim expression told him she wasn't joking.

His jaw dropped.

"You mean you . . ." He cleared his throat, which had gone hoarse. "You have sex with each of the three men?"

"It's not really having sex with *each* of the men as much as with *all* of them. Sometimes separate. Sometimes together."

Jealousy raged through him at the thought of Harmony in

another man's arms. Men. Other men touching her, making love to her. Several at the same time.

His cock twitched.

"The women, too," she continued. "Whatever permutation you can think of, we do it. Not that I'm bi, mind you, but when there are three . . . or four . . . or more of us together, we just do what comes naturally."

His breaths came in shallow tugs as adrenaline pumped through him at the sudden image of Harmony kissing another woman, of the two of them stroking each other and . . . His cock pushed painfully at his jeans.

"And it comes naturally to you to make love with other women?"

The thought of Harmony stroking another woman's breasts, of another woman kissing down Harmony's stomach, heading for those delicate black curls sent his cock pulsing.

"Look, Aiden, I'm not kidding myself that any of this seems natural to you. I know it's probably very unsettling to you and you probably want to run out of here right now and never see me again. You probably think that I'm a . . . that I . . ."

She was absolutely correct that he felt like running away right now—mostly from the confused feelings sweeping through him. He wasn't sure what he thought of the situation. He couldn't believe the woman he'd proposed to last night . . . a woman he thought he'd known so well . . . could actually be involved in an annual orgy.

From the look of her, he realized she was totally convinced

this would drive him away. Although he would need some time to get used to the idea . . . to readjust his thinking . . . he knew he still wanted her in his life.

"It's okay, sweetheart. I don't think less of you."

She swept a tear from her eye and gazed up at him. "But you are shocked."

That he couldn't deny. "What you just told me does defy everything I thought I knew about you, but that doesn't mean I love you less. I just have to get used to the idea, that's all."

She nodded then pushed herself to her feet. "I understand if you want to withdraw your proposal."

He grabbed her hand and drew her toward him.

"You're not getting away that easily. I still want to marry you . . . the question still stands . . ." He gazed into her eyes and smiled. "Will you marry me?"

Harmony stared at Aiden, amazed that he still wanted her to be his wife. She'd been certain he would march away in disgust, yet here he was . . . a little shaken, but still ready to make an honest woman of her.

She wanted to accept his proposal—to grasp the lifeline of normalcy and uprightness he had thrown her.

But she couldn't.

As much as he thought, here in Buffalo, where everything was proper and normal, that he could accept her annual activities, she didn't think he really comprehended the reality of it. And she didn't think he could really accept her if he did.

And the bottom line was, she wasn't sure she wanted to give it up.

"What if I told you that I wanted to keep going on these annual vacations?"

Aiden stared at her a moment and scratched his chin.

"Well, I guess I'd say that that would be fine. As long as I could go along, too."

THREE

That night, as Aiden pulled off his shirt and tossed it into the wicker laundry hamper in his bathroom, a fog of depression crept through him. He wished Harmony had accepted his proposal. He hated being in this limbo of not knowing.

His heart ached. He loved Harmony and he wanted to marry her. He also desperately wanted her to love him.

Mia had delayed responding to his proposal, and then broken his heart by deciding to run off with another guy instead. It had been tough getting over her—if he truly had at all. Mia had told him many times she loved him back, yet in the end she'd still left him. What if Harmony did the same thing?

He tugged off his socks and tossed them in behind the shirt. The important thing was that Harmony hadn't said no. It wasn't that she didn't love him. Her hesitation was tied to her insecurity about how he would react to her revelation about her yearly vacation.

He wondered if he'd been a complete idiot to suggest he accompany Harmony on one of her adventures. He walked into the bedroom and unfastened his jeans, then sat on the side of the bed. When she'd told him about the sexual aspect of her yearly trip, at first jealousy had flared through him, but that had quickly turned to a gut-gnawing lust as she'd described the activities in a little more detail. She hadn't even been talking in explicit terms, just that she'd been with men . . . more than one at a time . . . and *women,* too!

His groin tightened just remembering the conversation. Okay, so he should be jealous. He shouldn't want other men touching Harmony. But on the other hand, he'd always prided himself on being open to new ideas. He loved Harmony. He trusted her judgment. Jealousy had faded the more he'd thought about it. After all, if she'd wanted to be with one of those men, she would have married one of them by now. Twelve years was a long time. Clearly, they got together for the sexual exhilaration.

She just wanted to have fun, and be open sexually.

He stood up and tugged off his jeans, then pulled back the covers and climbed into bed. He realized that a part of him was still hung up because he viewed Harmony as a sweet, innocent type, when in fact, she was a woman with some very interesting experiences under her belt. The memory of her lips around his cock . . . of the dirty words she'd uttered to spur him along . . . sent his pulse vibrating.

"*Fuck me, baby,*" she'd demanded. "*I want you deep inside me.*"

So why the hell had she taken so long to show her wild side?

Aiden watched as Harmony beckoned to him, enticing him forward. A deep longing surged through him.

"Come here, Aiden. I need you."

She unzipped her long, turquoise velvet dress, revealing the swell of her breasts. She dropped the garment to the floor and stepped out of it, now standing totally naked in front of him.

His gaze locked on her naked pussy. He longed to reach out and pull her into his arms and glide his hard cock into her hot, moist depths.

Her hands stroked over her breasts, then one hand slid over her belly and between her thighs.

"Fuck me, baby." She sat down on the bed behind her, her soft, ivory skin a sharp contrast to the black velvet bedspread.

"No, fuck me."

He glanced sideways toward the new feminine voice. Mia stood in the doorway to this luxurious bedroom. She wore a long crimson dress of shiny satin that clung to every curve. Her breasts swelled from the strapless top. She strolled toward him, a confident smile on her lips.

His heart ached at the sight of her. He'd missed her for so long.

"It's me you want, Aiden." She stroked her satin-gloved fingers through his hair. Her soft touch sent heat spiraling through him.

"Aiden, fuck me," Harmony insisted. He glanced back to her naked, alluring form. God, he wanted her.

Mia, her face drawn tight in irritation, stood up and tore her dress off as she strode toward Harmony. Aiden's pulse accelerated as he watched Mia standing over Harmony in nothing but red stiletto heels and long red satin gloves. As he watched, Mia's shape quivered, then transformed. Now she was a strong, muscular man. Totally naked. She—or rather, he—knelt in front of Harmony and stroked along her thigh. Harmony sighed and opened her legs. The man leaned forward and licked one of Harmony's taut nipples, then the other.

"Oh, please fuck me," Harmony cried, her fingers slipping into her glistening slit.

The man's mouth captured Harmony's and she clung to his broad shoulders. His hand covered Harmony's, then his fingers slid inside her.

"Oh, yes . . . oh, yes . . ." Harmony gasped. "God, I'm coming."

Her body convulsed and she cried out as the man stroked inside her. When Harmony collapsed on the bed, the man pushed himself to his feet, his cock standing straight up, then drew Harmony to her feet. With his hands on her hips, he turned her around to face the bed. He urged her to lean over, then he positioned his cock against her ass. Slowly, he pushed forward, the long, hard cock disappearing into her back opening.

Aiden never thought he'd be attracted to a man, but this Mia-man had Aiden's cock pulsing.

"I'm fucking Harmony for you, Aiden." The man smiled over his shoulder, and he was Mia again. "Come and fuck me."

Mesmerized by the erotic sight of Mia, somehow with a cock inserted firmly in Harmony, he stood up and approached her, his throat dry. His cock throbbed with need. Mia shifted a little, sending the muscles in her buttocks rippling. Aiden's hands moved over her firm, round ass, then over Harmony's hip. He wrapped his arms around her—them—and cupped Harmony's breast.

"Fuck my ass, Aiden," Mia insisted. Her fingers danced up his chest as she leaned forward more. Her behind, round and enticing, tempted him.

"Do it, Aiden," Harmony said. "Fuck her."

"I want that cock of yours inside me," Mia murmured as her hand grasped him. She drew it to her hot opening.

Aiden arched his hips, his cock pressed against her warm ass. He grasped his erection and nudged it forward, positioning the tip against her opening.

"Oh, yeah, that's right," Mia encouraged.

His cock head slipped into her incredibly tight passage. It grasped him like a tight, hot fist.

"Push it right in, honey." Mia pushed back against him.

His cock slid in deeper. Unable to hold back, he thrust forward.

Both women moaned. He drew back and thrust forward again.

"Fuck me, baby," Mia said.

His cock pulsed.

"Fuck me, Aiden," Harmony cried.

It was like he was fucking both of them. Like Mia's cock was an extension of his own. In fact, he could feel it as if it was his own. A second cock giving him pleasure. And giving Harmony pleasure.

"Fuck me," Harmony insisted. "Fuck me harder."

He slid his hand down to her pussy and slipped between her lips. Mia's fingers joined his and they both entered Harmony.

As he held both women in his arms, he thrust again and again, filling them both with his cocks. He could feel them both clutch his cocks with their tight openings.

His groin tightened and pleasure shot through him as he erupted inside them.

"Yes, Aiden. Oh, God." Harmony gasped, then cried out in ecstasy.

Mia wailed in orgasm.

Finally, the three of them collapsed in a heap on the bed. The combination of the velvet bedspread and the satin skin of their bodies took his breath away. He stroked Mia's round breasts and leaned forward to kiss Harmony deeply.

The flight from Miami to St. Monterey in the Caribbean had been bumpy. Harmony pressed her hand across her temple as she and Aiden stepped from the gate into the busy terminal and followed the other passengers to the luggage carousel.

"Headache?" Aiden asked.

She nodded as she reached into her bag for the bottle of

painkillers she kept on hand, even though she hardly ever took them. When she got a headache like this, she liked to head it off before it got too bad.

She found a water fountain and swallowed the two white, oval pills as Aiden grabbed a luggage cart and rolled it toward the carousel. Passengers from a previous flight were still collecting their baggage. Harmony feared they might have a while to wait.

Aiden placed his hand on the small of her back.

"Don't worry. Once you get out into the sunshine, you'll feel better."

She glanced through the sliding doors of the terminal and the sight of palm trees and rich blue skies did brighten her mood. It had been snowing when they'd left Buffalo, with a promise of ten inches to come.

Aiden took her carry-on bag and placed it beside his on the cart.

"Honey, why don't you go sit on that bench over there while I call for the resort shuttle." He pointed to a wooden bench not far from the doors and out of the thick of the crowd.

She nodded and headed for the bench with the cart. Her headache seemed to be easing off, until she thought about Aiden checking into the resort and running into Jake or Trey . . . or Cole. Oh, man, she wasn't ready for this.

She sighed and stroked both temples.

A few minutes later, Aiden sat down beside her.

"The shuttle will be here in fifteen minutes." His arm slid around her waist. "Still not feeling better?"

OPAL CAREW

She shook her head and leaned against his shoulder. She liked having him here. He'd sensed her nervousness when the flight got bumpy and chatted with her, successfully keeping her mind off the turbulence most of the time.

The carousel started and the ramp carried the luggage downward. Passengers pushed in closer, several grabbing bags and pulling them off the machine. Harmony noticed her large burgundy suitcase appear at the top of the ramp.

"You sit. I'll go get the luggage."

He'd arranged for the taxi to the airport and now he'd taken charge of getting their baggage and getting them to the resort. Not that she couldn't do those things on her own, but it was nice not having to.

A few minutes later, they stepped outside into the bright sunshine. A warm breeze caressed her cheek and she realized her headache had dissipated.

Soon a small, white bus pulled up in front of them with the resort name, HIDDEN PARADISE, written along the side in a bright design of red, orange, and hot pink.

They climbed aboard and Aiden tucked his arm around her waist as the driver pulled away. Harmony watched the lovely view outside the window. Palm trees. Tropical foliage. A nearly cloudless, bright blue sky.

The trip passed quickly and soon they stood at the front desk in the light and airy lobby of the luxury resort. People in shorts and bathing suits milled around them as a bellman rolled a huge cart of luggage toward the elevators. Harmony could see the ocean out the large windows on the other side of the lobby. Seagulls floated lazily in the distance and the sand on the beach looked white and warm. She could barely wait to sink her toes into it.

Aiden finished checking in and handed her a large, brown envelope with her name scrawled on the front.

"This was waiting for you."

She nodded. "This will give us some details about where and when to meet the others, and some of the facilities that have been set up for us."

Suddenly, her headache was back.

Harmony slid the key card into the slot and pushed the door open. Aiden followed her, carrying the suitcases. Harmony glanced around as she stepped into the room. The soft furnishings were in neutral beiges, with liberal splashes of bright reds and oranges, and the couch and armchairs formed a cozy sitting area by the patio doors. She crossed the room to the window and glanced outside. A large balcony with a table and chairs overlooked a beautiful ocean vista. The clear aquamarine water shone like a jewel in the sunlight.

"Nice view," Aiden said as he peered out behind her. "In fact, the whole place is really great."

"These are bigger than the normal rooms. The person who makes the arrangements for these trips—a sister of one of the group members, I think—gets us a special deal."

Aiden turned the dead bolt on the door to the adjoining room, then pulled it open and stepped through, still carrying his suitcase. He dropped it inside then strolled back into Harmony's room.

"That one is just as nice. Tell me again why I'm in a separate room."

"It's one to a room for everyone," Harmony answered as she pulled her red cocktail dress from her suitcase and hung it in the closet. "It works better that way." She scooped up her three bikinis and dropped them into the top drawer of the dresser. "That gives everyone the freedom to get away from everything and everyone if they want to."

Harmony was glad for the buffer. If Aiden didn't take well to Harmony's *activities* with her friends, they could keep some space between them. She just hoped he wouldn't want that space to be permanent . . . as in breaking up.

He skimmed his hands around her waist and kissed her neck. "But I don't want to get away from you."

She smiled and turned toward him. He was so sweet. Maybe she should never have risked their relationship by telling him about these trips of hers . . . but she knew she couldn't hide this side of herself from him. Not if they were to have a future together. Better to bare all, so to speak, and let him decide.

Even if that decision was to leave her.

She wrapped her arms around him and kissed him soundly . . . holding him maybe a little too tightly and a little too long . . . then released him and went to gather her four pairs of sandals and place them in the bottom drawer.

"So how's this going to work with me?" Aiden asked,

leaning against the edge of the desk and watching her. "Am I basically going to be sitting alone in my room while you're in here entertaining one guy after another?"

She lifted her floral linen skirt from the suitcase and shook it out, then walked to the closet and picked out a hanger with clips on it.

"No, I told you, you're welcome to join in."

She glanced in her suitcase at the lacy thongs, garter belts and bras, her favorite leather basque, and sundry other sexy items. She scooped up what she could and tugged open the middle dresser drawer, tossing the lot inside.

"So that means you and me and some other guy in a threesome?"

Her stomach twisted. If she and Aiden wound up in a three-some . . . no, *when* they wound up in a threesome . . . would she see a look of disgust on his face afterward? Aimed at her.

She pushed away her anxieties as she walked toward the end of the bed and sat down. She had invited him here, so there was no backing off now.

"You don't have to limit your activities to being with me." She smiled. "Well, as long as Nikki and Angela approve of you." She patted the bed beside her and he came over to sit. "And knowing them as I do . . ." She dragged her index finger down his broad, muscular chest. ". . . and the way you look . . ." She toyed with his top button. "Especially with your shirt off . . . I'm sure there'll be no problem there."

"So you're really saying you don't mind me taking one of these women up to my room and having sex with her."

"One . . . or both." She winked. "Or all three of us."

He grinned. "I think I'm going to like this."

He stood up and plucked a sheer purple teddy from her suitcase and held it up, a big smile on his face. "I think you missed this." He tugged open the drawer where she'd put her lingerie and dropped the teddy inside.

She shuddered. At some point, given the way these weeks usually went, he would see her with another man—or more—actually in the act.

Oh, well, she'd face that situation when she came to it.

For now, she'd stay focused on getting settled in. Her stomach twisted. She wasn't even sure if she'd be able to go through with any of the usual activities with Aiden here.

For so long, she'd kept these two parts of her life separate. They were like two different worlds. One in which she was a staid, responsible woman who managed an office for a small insurance firm and the other where she was a shameless vixen who participated in wild, outrageous sex.

Aiden was part of her everyday world. She glanced around at the luxurious suite, then out the window at the palm trees swaying in the ocean breeze and the blue sky beyond. This was her fantasy world. With Aiden here, her two worlds had come crashing together—and she wasn't quite sure how to deal with it.

FOUR

Harmony walked hand in hand with Aiden along the walk-way toward the large, free-form pool. A beautiful backdrop of rocks with a waterfall glittering in the sunlight and a sur-rounding stone patio gave the pool a natural feel. She breathed in the salty ocean air and smiled. This was such a welcome change from the snowy weather back home.

"Beautiful, isn't it?"

"You bet." Aiden smiled and squeezed her hand. "Almost as beautiful as you."

He opened the decorative wrought-iron gate and held it for her as she passed through, then they strolled to the side of the pool. There were only a few people here—some loung-ing on chairs reading or catching rays, and several in the wa-ter.

She dropped her bright floral towel and straw bag on one of the blue lounge chairs across from the waterfall, which fed into the pool. Aiden dropped his towel, one of the plain white ones supplied by the resort, on the chair beside hers.

The sun heated her skin as she peeled off her sarong and dropped it over the back of the chair. The burble of the splashing water relaxed her coiled nerves.

"I'm going for a dip. You coming?" Aiden asked.

"No, I think I'll just relax and work on my tan."

She tugged her sunglasses from her bag and put them on, then sat down and watched Aiden as he unbuttoned his shirt. His hard, firm muscles rippled as he slid it off his shoulders and dropped it on the chair next to her. He strolled to the diving board and did a perfect jackknife dive. She noticed several of the women around the pool watching him with avid interest, too.

She pulled her book from her bag and settled back in the chair, her broad-rimmed straw hat shading her eyes from the bright sun. As she opened her book, her gaze drifted to a tall, muscular man settling on a lounge chair across the pool. His sandy-colored hair was short and stylishly tousled with blond highlights.

It was Trey.

She tensed. He hadn't seen her yet and she hoped he wouldn't. She wasn't ready to face anyone from the group right now. It wasn't just because it would be the first time Aiden would come face-to-face with one of the group members—a *male* member—but also because she wasn't quite ready to become that other woman. That lascivious woman she became every year.

Trey glanced around and she lifted the book higher to cover her face. She could still see him, but she was hoping between the book, the sunglasses, and the brim of her hat, he wouldn't notice her.

No such luck.

He glanced her way and smiled, then headed in her direction.

"Well, hello there, beautiful."

As he smiled down at her, sunlight glinted from his ear. Trey's trademark diamond stud earring.

She lowered her book. He certainly was a stunning example of manhood. The evidence of his healthy lifestyle showed in every rippling muscle on his arms and shoulders, his tight, ridged stomach, his contoured legs. He liked to cycle and typically rode to work every day and often did long cycling trips on weekends. He even had a home gym in his basement and in the winter, he skied.

"Trey." She smiled.

"May I join you?"

"Well, I . . ." She glanced toward the pool and saw Aiden swimming laps. He wouldn't be done for another ten minutes at least. But that didn't matter. She had nothing to hide. "Of course. It's nice to see you again."

"So formal. How about a hug?"

He plucked her hat from her head, then scooped her into his arms and hugged her close to his solid . . . and quite bare . . . chest. The feel of her breasts pressed against his naked skin sent shivers through her. An image of his long, rigid cock gliding in and out of her flashed through her brain. He kissed her, his lips caressing hers in his playful way. Then his tongue slid between her lips, and hers tangled against his in a natural response.

She knew Trey. She'd known him for a long time. Her body welcomed him.

He eased away and smiled at her with great warmth.

"Oh, man, I've missed you." He released her, but his arm remained tucked around her waist.

Aiden pushed his wet hair out of his eyes and glanced over to the chair where Harmony sat . . . and he froze.

Some guy was kissing his woman.

Aiden climbed out of the pool, water streaming down his body, and stormed across the stone deck.

The guy eased away from Harmony, but he kept his arm around her, holding her close like he'd known her forever. As Aiden approached them, he realized maybe that was true. This guy was probably one of the infamous group of six.

Suddenly, Aiden wasn't quite so sure about the soundness of his decision to come here.

"Harmony, who's your friend?" Aiden asked as he stepped up beside her.

The guy glanced up and Harmony turned her head in Aiden's direction. She stepped back, putting a little distance between herself and the man.

"Oh, this is—"

"Trey." Trey leaned forward and offered his hand, a friendly smile on his face. "You must be Aiden."

Aiden shook hands with him, not quite sure he liked the guy.

"You're a lucky man," Trey continued. "Harmony is a special woman."

Aiden slid his arm around her possessively and drew her close to his body.

"Yes, she is."

"Aiden, are you sure you're going to be able to cope with this?" Harmony asked as they stepped onto the elevator.

She had seen the jealousy in his eyes when he'd seen her with Trey and the possessive way he'd pulled her against his side to show Trey exactly whose woman she was.

She was already wondering how she was going to cope herself. Seeing Trey—being touched by Trey—had thrown her totally off balance, reminding her of erotic encounters and wild sexual escapades. Her body thrummed with heat.

But Aiden practically had steam spurting from his ears when he'd seen Trey and Harmony together. How was he ever going to cope with seeing her actually having sex with another man?

"It just caught me off guard, that's all."

He pushed the button to the fourteenth floor and the

doors slid closed. They were alone in the elevator and she became conscious of his sexy, naked torso, bulging with muscles. His solid masculinity. His musky scent.

"You know, I still love *you,* no matter what I've done . . ." She sidled closer to him, her arm brushing his, causing electricity to course through her. ". . . or will do . . . with these other men."

His intent gaze burned through her. "I like hearing you say you love me."

She stroked her finger down his arm.

"Would you like me to show you just how much I love you?" Her finger swirled around his ear, then down his chest. Lower . . . and lower. . . .

"I'd like that very much."

She slid her fingertip along the waistband of his swimming trunks, then slipped her finger under the left side and dipped inside until she felt the flat, hard key card he had tucked in the inside pocket. She tugged it out, then opened the small silver door on the elevator panel and pushed the card into the slot there. She pushed the red STOP button beside the slot and the elevator came to a halt.

"What did you do?" he asked.

She grinned. "The person I told you about who makes the arrangements for these group vacations has some interesting connections. In addition to getting us a great deal, she always arranges for us to have special access at the resorts we go to. Our key cards allow us to put elevators on service, to access the health club after hours, etcetera."

She reached behind her neck and untied her bikini strap.

Aiden's groin tightened as he realized what Harmony intended.

"Really?"

His gaze followed her every move with anticipation. She dropped the halter straps and the triangles of fabric that hid her breasts fell straight down, revealing her round white mounds, the nipples puckering into tight pebbles.

"How do you feel about some hot, sweaty sex in an elevator?"

Like my favorite fantasy has just come true!

She stepped toward him and wrapped her arms around his neck, pressing her nipples into his naked chest as her breasts crushed against him.

"I think I might just like this trip after all."

He slid his hands along her silky back, then drew her tightly against him, his blood simmering at the feel of her hot, nearly naked body pressed the length of his.

On an elevator.

He captured her lips and drove his tongue into her hot, moist mouth, just like he wanted to do with his cock into her hot, wet pussy.

"Oh, Aiden," she murmured, a breathless catch to her voice. She clutched his hand and pressed it to her breast, then moaned as he squeezed her, then tweaked her nipple. "Suck my breast. Take it in your mouth and pull on it so hard I cry out."

Oh God, she was sexy. His cock twitched as he leaned down and licked her hard, throbbing nipple. She moaned.

"Suck it, baby. Suck it hard."

He drew it into his mouth and sucked, his hand firm against her back, holding her close. He licked the tip, swirling his tongue around it, then sucked again.

Her fingers dipped into her bikini bottom and slid back and forth, then she drew them out and smeared her slippery essence over her other nipple. Oh, man, she was being so incredibly sexy. He breathed in the sweet, honey scent of her as he lapped at her nipple, then sucked on it hungrily.

He backed her against the side of the elevator and pinned her flat against the wall as he sucked first one nipple, then the other. He pressed her breasts together, bringing the nipples closer, then shifted his mouth from nipple to nipple, the tight nubs brushing against his tongue, until she wailed in pleasure. He licked one hard nub, then spiraled his tongue around it. Her aureole was hard and distended, eagerly pushing into his mouth. He shifted to the other one and flicked his tongue back and forth on it, then sucked it in a gentle pulsing rhythm. Her fingers spiked through his hair and she moaned in pleasure.

He kissed down her belly to her bikini bottoms. She tugged on the string holding the sides together, releasing one side, then the other. The scrap of fabric fell to the floor, leaving her silken pussy, which had been waxed into a neat little landing strip of black curls, naked to his gaze.

He smiled in delight.

"That is adorable." He stroked the little row of soft fur

with his fingertip, then drew her folds apart with his thumbs and dove in with his tongue.

At the feel of Aiden's tongue caressing her slit, Harmony gasped with pleasure. He dabbed at her clit and she forked her fingers through his hair, holding him to her. He nuzzled, then swirled his tongue around and around. Pleasure beat through her like the pounding of primitive drums. When he sucked on her . . .

"Oh, God, Aiden. Yes. *Yes!*"

Joy pulsed through her, then swelled in a wild surge of bliss—and erupted into ecstasy.

Her knees went weak and she sank to the floor. Desperate for Aiden's cock, she reached for his trunks and tugged them downward, catching his gigantic erection as it bounced forward. She wrapped her lips around him and sucked him deep into her mouth.

Aiden groaned. The feel of her mouth embracing his cock—of being so intimately connected with her—sent heat through his body. Not just because of the erotic sensations, but because he loved her . . . and loved being this way with her.

Their lovemaking sessions had always been gentle and loving—until the night of his proposal when they'd gotten a little wild and crazy, but still nothing like this tempestuous session.

He had sensed she'd still been holding herself back and now he realized just how much.

He still couldn't believe they were having sex *in an elevator.*

Excitement coiled through him as her mouth moved up and down his cock, her tongue swirling around him . . . then she nipped lightly. She grazed her teeth along his shaft, then kissed the tip. She dove forward, swallowing him down her throat, then sucked hard.

Her fingers curled around his balls and stroked, sending his heart pumping harder. He tried not to think about the fact that it was this place that was bringing out her sexy beast . . . in fact, probably that man, Trey.

As she stroked his perineum and pleasure pummeled his groin, he realized whatever was causing it, he should be thankful.

"Come here, sweetheart," he said as he held out his hands to her. He wanted to be inside her when he came.

Harmony released his cock from between her lips and kissed the tip. She clasped his hands and pulled herself to her feet, then wrapped her arms around his shoulders as he nudged his cock-head between her thighs.

She opened her legs and he lifted her. His cock slid into her, gliding along her sensitive walls, stretching her with his girth. She squeezed him tight inside her, welcoming him, as she wrapped her legs around his waist and crossed her ankles behind his back, allowing his cock to drive deeper into her. He drew back and thrust forward, pressing her against the side of the elevator.

Her eyes rolled back and she groaned.

He thrust again and again, banging her against the wall,

intense pleasure skyrocketing through her. She sucked in air as the pleasure mounted, pummeling her with wild excitement.

"More, baby. Harder," she insisted.

He rammed harder, driving her to exhilarating heights of bliss, then . . .

"Oh, yeah . . ." she whimpered. "I'm coming."

He kissed her neck, sending tingles dancing along her skin, as he continued thumping into her. Pleasure blazed over her, then washed through every cell as she wailed in a long, languorous release. On and on . . . his hard cock still inside her. She felt him stiffen and jerk, signaling his climax.

She held him tight against her, squeezing him inside her as he rode his release. When he relaxed against her, she stroked his back, wondering what he thought about seeing this side of her. He nuzzled her neck, then kissed her ear.

"That was pretty sensational," he murmured.

She uncoiled her legs and pressed her toes to the floor as he eased away from her. She smiled as she forked her fingers through her hair and pushed it back.

"It *was* pretty great."

Aiden smiled at her. She was so beautiful with her tousled black hair billowing out around her face, her cheeks rosy from their passion, her eyes twinkling. Of course, seeing her totally naked, aside from her bikini top, which still dangled beneath her breasts, was quite a turn-on. Her lovely breasts rising and falling with her breath. The tuft of black fur on her pussy. Even though he'd just had her, he'd love to do it all over again.

Other men are going to make love to my woman . . . but it's okay.

Aiden repeated the mantra as he dressed for dinner.

"You look very handsome."

Harmony stood in the bedroom doorway, stunning in a royal blue, glittery dress that hugged every curve and lifted her breasts forward as though offering them to him. The fabric cascaded to the floor like a waterfall, pooling around her feet.

"That's some dress."

He was torn between wanting her to change into something less revealing, knowing every man who saw her would want her—and three would get their wish—and wanting to watch her walk and dance in that enchanting garment.

She stepped forward, her hips swaying in an enticing manner, then she twirled, sending flickering light scattering around the room.

"I'm glad you like it." She kissed his cheek then curled her arm around his.

Riding in the elevator again reminded Aiden of what he and Harmony had done a mere two hours ago. He loved to see this wild, uninhibited side of her—so different from what he'd always believed about her.

The elevator stopped a couple floors down and the other people got off. After the doors closed, he slipped his arm around Harmony's waist and drew her in close to his body. Why had she wanted to hide this side of herself?

"Harmony, I'm not really sure I understand why you held off showing me what you're really like for so long."

She glanced down at her hands, which clung tightly to her silver sequined evening bag.

"I was afraid you might not like . . . you know . . . how I am in bed."

He raised an eyebrow. "You're kidding, right?"

She glanced at him from under her eyelashes and shook her head. "I'm never really sure how to act with regular guys."

"Regular?"

"Anyone other than Jake, or Trey, or Cole. With them I can do anything I want . . . they won't judge me."

"You thought I'd judge you?"

She pursed her lips.

"It's more like I was afraid I might go too far. Step out of the bounds of your comfort zone."

"And then I'd break up with you over it?"

He was disappointed that she believed that of him.

She nodded, but he sensed more. A flicker of pain . . . almost fear.

"Harmony, did something happen in the past . . . did you push someone's limits and he reacted badly?"

Her gaze flicked away.

"You could say that. I let my guard down . . . sort of fell into how I am here . . . you know a little more open . . . a little crazy . . ."

He didn't like the trapped look on her face, the stiffness of her back, the way she leaned away from him, as if seeking escape.

"You find you're different on these vacations than when you're back home?"

"Of course. I always hold myself back when I'm in my regular life. I wouldn't want people to know how I am here."

"Why?"

She stared at him. "Because it's . . . not exactly how most people behave."

"You don't have to be like everyone else."

"Of course I do. People judge you . . . People . . ." Her eyes glimmered and he wondered just what *people* had done to her.

"Why don't you tell me about what happened with this guy?"

FIVE

Anger simmered through Aiden at the thought of some guy treating Harmony badly. Harmony stared at her freshly polished, glossy red fingernails.

"I'd been dating him for a while and we were making love in his apartment—by the fireplace—when his roommate came home. We didn't realize at first, you know, because we were . . ."

She glanced at him, trying to look nonchalant, but failing miserably. Her lower lip quivered as she spoke and her whole face was drawn tight.

"But when we did, we noticed he had his . . . well, he was enjoying what he saw. I was really turned on and . . . thought nothing of it at the time . . . but I asked him if he wanted to join us. He jumped right in. The guy I was with was hesitant at first, but once things got going, he seemed to be enjoying it."

"Until?"

Her fingers clenched tightly around her bag, her knuckles almost white. "The next morning, after his roommate had left for work . . . my boyfriend . . . he . . ." She sucked in a deep breath. "Didn't behave very well."

"The jackass."

She shrugged. "That's how most people think, isn't it? There's a line you don't cross." She sighed. "The way I behave here is different from how I am at home. Sometimes I slip . . . show a little of how I am here. After that incident, I decided to keep a tight rein on myself. I worried that it would happen again. That people would judge me. I even started to think maybe I should pull away from the group, but I've known these people for a long time . . . I care about them. I'm not sure what life would be like without this wild, wonderful time away from the everyday. So I couldn't decide to quit, but I didn't want to take a chance on the way I behave here seeping into the way I behave there. I just happened to meet you right after I made that decision."

He stroked his hands over her shoulders, then drew her into his arms. "That guy was a total jackass and it's too bad his narrow-minded behavior has affected how you feel about yourself. There's nothing wrong with being open and uninhibited."

"Tell me that again after the week is done," she murmured.

He realized she had brought him here as a test . . . to see if he would judge her. A test she seemed sure he'd fail.

Aiden accompanied Harmony across the softly lit ballroom. Men in well-tailored suits and women in stylish long dresses milled about, looking for empty tables or chatting in groups with drinks in their hands as soft music played in the background. Since guests typically came to Hidden Paradise for a week at a time, starting on the weekend, the resort held a welcome party every Saturday so the guests could kick off their vacation with a night of dinner, dancing, and fun.

"Hey, Harmony. Over here."

A man at a table with several other people waved his hand. At first it looked like his light brown hair was short and brushed back off his face, then Aiden realized it was actually pulled back and tied behind his head.

"That's Jake," Harmony murmured in his ear. She drew Aiden in the direction of the table.

Aiden noticed the sandy-haired man with the diamond earring from the pool—Trey—was also at the table. There were also two beautiful women, one a brunette with her hair piled high on her head in a swirl of curls and the other a blonde with a bright smile and her hair pinned back.

Jake stood up and gave Harmony a big hug. Aiden noticed his hand slip over her backside and give a slight squeeze, but Aiden clamped down the jealousy surging through him.

Other men are going to make love to my woman . . . but it's okay.

When would he start believing that?

Jake gestured for them to sit down at the table. Actually, it was a large oval booth with a couple of chairs on the open side. Everyone slid around so that Harmony could sit on the upholstered bench and Aiden slid in beside her. Quite cozy.

Maybe a little too cozy, he thought, with Harmony pushed up so close beside Jake.

"So this is your boyfriend." Jake held out his hand and Aiden shook it. "Nice to meet you, Aiden. You've already met Trey, I hear."

Aiden nodded to the other man.

"This is Angela." He gestured to the blonde who sat on the chair, then to the brunette. "And this is Nicole, but we all call her Nikki."

"Delighted," Aiden said, smiling. Nikki had amazing blue eyes and a gorgeous mass of curls tumbling from the jeweled clip on top of her head, accentuating her long, graceful neck. Angela's green eyes lit up her heart-shaped face when she smiled. And from what he could see of their figures . . . Nikki's deep cleavage was showcased by the plunging halter-style blue dress she wore, and the red sequined fabric of Angela's dress strained across her bosom . . . Wow!

Other men are going to make love to my woman . . . but it's okay.

And it's okay for me to have sex with these women!

So far at the table there were three women, including Harmony, and three men, including himself. Which meant one man was missing.

"Someone's still coming?" he asked Harmony.

She nodded. "Cole's not here yet."

The waiter came by and took Harmony and Aiden's drink order and left them two dinner menus. Soon the waiter brought their drinks. A Passion Fruit Fling for Harmony and an imported beer for Aiden. He poured the amber liquid from the green bottle into the tall-stemmed glass the waiter had brought, then took a swig.

"Look, there's Cole," Angela said as she smiled and waved at someone across the room.

Aiden glanced around and saw a man with black hair skimming his collar approach the table. Both Angela and Nikki got up and gave him a hug.

The newcomer smiled at Harmony.

"Hello, Cole," she said, almost shyly.

"How're you doing, dream girl?" His smile showed even white teeth and, although Aiden wasn't into guys, he could tell this guy was a good-looking man.

Cole took Harmony's hand and kissed it. Aiden could almost detect a slight blush along her cheeks.

With this many people involved, each was bound to have a favorite. This Cole guy was obviously hers.

"So you must be Aiden." Cole shook Aiden's hand with a firm grip then sat down on the chair beside him and next to Angela.

Even though Aiden was between Cole and Harmony, he still felt they were too close.

The waiter came by and took their orders, then lit the two candles in the center of the table. The music continued to play through the meal.

"So what do you do, Aiden?" Nikki asked as the waiter picked up an empty plate.

"I'm an architect. I specialize in energy-efficient, environmentally friendly design." He smiled. "What about you?"

"I'm a high school teacher. I teach chemistry and math." She picked up her wine glass and took a sip.

He could just imagine a hoard of wide-eyed teenage boys all racing for the front row in her classes.

"I'm a waste disposal engineer," Angela said.

Harmony nudged his elbow and laughed. "She likes to say that. You think she means she rides on the back of a garbage truck and picks up trash bags on the street, right?"

"Do you?" Aiden asked.

Angela grinned. "Actually, I work for a company that has developed a new way to dispose of garbage. They use a plasma torch to super heat it without burning until it breaks down into its component elements. The main product is a very clean natural gas and the other products are all environmentally friendly."

"Impressive."

Harmony was pleased that Aiden seemed to be fitting into the group well. And he seemed to be enjoying himself.

She glanced at Cole as he sipped his wine. He caught her

gaze and sent her a quick smile and a wink. Her heart thumped. He looked so good. Glossy black hair sweeping back from his face in waves, full lips, and that adorable twinkle in his eye when he smiled. He wasn't as classically handsome as Aiden, nor as tall, but he was still hot.

She remembered when they'd first met in college. It was freshman year and Cole had pulled a practical joke on Trey and Jake and they'd been chasing him across the campus. Harmony had been walking along the path toward the psychology building when Cole raced around the corner and ran smack into her, flinging her flat on her butt on the grass and sending her books flying. Laughing and out of breath, he picked himself up from the ground and apologized profusely as he took her hand and helped her to her feet. Trey and Jake suddenly appeared, knocking both Cole and Harmony to the ground again.

The three guys had insisted on buying her a coffee at the student center to apologize and they'd chatted for an hour or so before Trey and Jake left for a late afternoon class. Cole had asked Harmony to join him for dinner. There had been a sizzling attraction between them and Harmony felt certain he would have asked her out if she hadn't been dating a boy back home. By the time she had ended it with her old beau, Cole was dating someone else. A close friendship formed between the two of them, then it seemed impossible to act on that attraction. Until the night the six of them had formed the group . . .

The waiter collected their dessert plates and brought

coffee and tea. The band began to play, starting with a sultry slow number.

"Harmony," Cole said, "would you care to dance?"

Harmony glanced at Aiden who nodded and stood up to let her out of the booth. He took her hand to help her out, then sat back down. His face gave no indication of his feelings, but she sensed a simmering jealousy.

Damn, she hoped she hadn't made a dire mistake bringing him here.

Cole took her hand and led her to the dance floor. As his arms came around her and he held her close to his body, she felt warmth whisper through her. She loved being in Cole's arms . . . looked forward to it every year. But this time it was different. She was worried about Aiden, whether he was jealous, if he was feeling insecure.

"He seems like a great guy," Cole said.

She nodded. "He is."

"The others seem to be okay with him. There should be no problem with him joining us for the week." He searched her face. "Or is there?"

"You mean, is he going to be jealous?"

He nodded.

"He says this is okay with him."

"But you're not so sure. You brought him here to see how he'd react, didn't you?"

She nodded. He knew her so well. She relaxed into his arms and floated across the floor, enjoying just being with him. No stress. No worry about what he was thinking. She knew Cole accepted her for exactly who she was. She didn't have to pretend with him.

Aiden watched Harmony and Cole on the dance floor, his stomach in a knot. Angela smiled at him and he decided to ask her to dance.

He leaned toward her. "Angela, would you—"

"Aiden?"

He jerked around at the familiar voice. He must be hearing things. But, no, there stood Mia, looking exceptionally beautiful in a form-fitting black gown that flared below her knees.

Mia. The woman he'd loved for three years. The woman who had dumped him a year and a half ago.

The woman he'd never quite gotten over.

SIX

Aiden stood up. "Mia, what are you doing here?"

The sight of her in a long black dress that accentuated her curves, her long auburn hair caressing her shoulders, took his breath away.

She smiled, but glanced at the group at the table uncertainly.

"I'm . . . on vacation."

Trey's gaze glided over her shapely form and an appreciative smile curled his lips.

"Aiden, why don't you invite your friend to join us?" he said.

Mia glanced at the people at the table.

"Are you sure it's all right?"

They all made sounds of assent, including the ladies. Mia glanced at Aiden for confirmation. He nodded.

"Everyone, this is Mia Jennings." He pulled out a chair for her as he introduced the people around the table.

Her woodsy, floral scent wafted past him as she sat down. Her arm brushed his and heat careened through him.

Why the hell was she here?

Everyone at the table introduced themselves and Aiden called the waiter over. Mia ordered a champagne cocktail. A memory of the two of them sharing a bottle of champagne at that little getaway they loved to go to in the Poconos skittered into his mind. How she'd taken a sip, then sucked his cock into her mouth. The cold, bubbly liquid had swirled against him as her warm tongue had danced over his cockhead.

He shifted in his seat, his pants now uncomfortably tight against his swelling member.

Harmony and Cole returned from the dance floor, both glancing at the stranger sitting at their table. Aiden stood up to let Harmony sit down, as Cole retrieved a chair from an empty table near them.

"Harmony," Aiden said, "this is Mia, a friend of mine from Buffalo." He omitted the fact they used to date. This wasn't the time or place. "Mia, this is my girlfriend, Harmony."

Harmony gazed at the newcomer. A friend from Buffalo and she showed up here? That was an odd coincidence.

Harmony smiled and held out her hand. "Nice to meet you."

The other woman hesitated a moment, then shook her hand. "Nice to meet you, Harmony."

This Mia was an exceptionally pretty woman, with deep blue eyes and auburn hair that fell in waves past her shoulders. Her clinging black dress suited her well and showed off a trim yet shapely figure.

Harmony noticed the way Aiden looked at her. The nervous way he toyed with his class ring, turning it from side to side on his finger.

"So how do you know each other?" she asked.

"Aiden's sister and I are old friends. She introduced us several years ago." Mia glanced around the table. "How do you all know each other?"

"We're old friends from college," Jake said. "We've been meeting every year since we graduated."

"Oh, you must be very close."

Trey grinned. "You have no idea."

Nikki leaned over to Trey and whispered in his ear. He smiled and nodded.

"Mia," he said, "would you like to dance?"

She smiled. "Sure."

Nikki stood up to let Trey out. As Trey led Mia to the dance floor, Nikki wrapped her hand around Aiden's arm.

He expected her to suggest they dance, but instead, she flashed him a seductive smile and said, "Why don't you come and sit with us for a bit?"

He glanced at Harmony and she just grinned. He slid over to the other side of the booth. Nikki whispered something to Jake and everyone reorganized themselves until Aiden was in the back of the booth with Harmony on one side and Nikki on the other. Firm female thighs pressed the length of his.

A warm, soft hand glided along his thigh—Nikki's—and came to rest within an inch of his rapidly growing cock. Nikki leaned toward Harmony, her breast brushing Aiden's arm.

"You certainly do have a sexy boyfriend."

Harmony smiled, her hands wrapped around her stemmed glass. "I think so."

Nikki's hand began to travel again and his breath caught as she slid over his hard cock. She snagged the tag of his zipper and drew it down. Good God, what was the woman doing? They were in public. Her fingers expertly slipped past layers of fabric until she came into contact with his naked flesh, then wrapped around his hard cock. He drew in a deep breath as her hand glided up, then down.

"Oh, I dropped my napkin," Angela said, and smiled as she sank beneath the table.

A second later, Aiden felt another pair of hands on his cock. He had *two* women handling his cock right here in public. Two beautiful, sexy women. No one could actually see, since the tablecloth hid everything, but someone might catch them.

Nikki's hand encircled him with warmth while Angela toyed with the tip. When he felt her warm mouth cover him, he had to suppress a groan. He glanced at Harmony, worried what she would think. She smiled knowingly and leaned toward him.

"It seems you have their seal of approval." She winked at Nikki.

Angela licked his cock-head, then swirled her tongue around the corona. The warm, wet sensation felt so good he could barely keep a straight face.

"I think Angela is having trouble down there. I'll go help her." Nikki disappeared under the table. A second later, a second pair of lips began to work on his cock, gliding up the side while Angela sucked the tip of him. He drew in a deep breath.

Harmony took his hand. He squeezed, trying to relieve the pressure of trying not to show any reaction to the intensely erotic sensations going on under the table. Of the warm, moist feminine mouths wrapped around his throbbing cock.

Angela released the tip, then she and Nikki positioned themselves on either side of his cock and caressed his shaft with their delicate lips, gliding up and down his length. They slipped off the end for a moment, and he thought they were kissing each other under the table. The thought of the two women, locked at the lips, possibly caressing each other's breasts, sent a new rush of desire through him. A moment later, one mouth sucked him deep inside, pulling then releasing, pulling then releasing. Heat surged through him. That mouth slipped off and the other took him inside. He felt fingers stroking his balls and a moment later, a tongue caressed them.

Oh, God, the attention of the two women was driving him mad.

"Relax and enjoy it," Harmony murmured in his ear. As his balls were drawn into a warm mouth and the other mouth sucked hard on his cock, he hung on a tightrope . . . until Harmony blew a whisper of air into his ear, then nuzzled his temple.

He tensed and groaned as his cock spewed into the warm dampness. The woman under the table sucked and licked as he spurted, then he slumped back in his seat. As his breathing calmed, he glanced around, expecting everyone to be staring at him, but other than Cole's wry grin and Harmony's hand tightening around his in a quick squeeze, everyone else in the ballroom totally ignored him. Of course, the lights were dim and the sound of the music would have drowned out his sounds.

Mia returned from the dance floor with Trey. Aiden blanched at the thought of what she would have seen if she'd shown up ten seconds ago.

"Where did everyone go?" she asked.

Aiden realized the table looked rather empty with just Harmony, Cole, and him visible. Jake seemed to have slipped away while Aiden was preoccupied, and the two women were still under the table.

As Mia and Trey sat down, the tablecloth flipped up beside him and Angela appeared, followed a few seconds later by Nikki.

"We found it," Nikki said as she held up a white cloth napkin.

Mia raised an eyebrow but said nothing. She glanced at Aiden questioningly. Something in his face must have given him away because her glance dashed to Harmony then ricocheted away. A faint flush stained Mia's cheeks.

What must she be thinking?

Trey started a discussion with Mia, his arm casually around her waist. Aiden's gaze locked on Trey's hand as it rested on her hip.

Aiden told himself it didn't matter, he and Mia were history, but the man's easy familiarity with her, his fingers lightly touching her, and the way he leaned in to murmur in her ear as they talked, bugged Aiden.

When she laughed, he gritted his teeth.

Harmony rested her hand on his arm and leaned in toward him. "So how do you like the group so far?"

He tugged his attention from Mia and Trey and gazed at Harmony's smiling face. What the hell was wrong with him? Harmony was the one he was here with.

Remembering the two women pleasuring him under the table, he smiled.

"They're pretty great."

He glanced at Trey and Mia.

Why the hell was she here, anyway? He found this situation stressful enough without having her adding to it. He needed to get to the bottom of it.

He kissed Harmony's cheek. "Do you mind if I ask Mia to dance with me?"

"No, of course not."

Harmony slid from the booth to let Aiden out. What was the relationship between Mia and Aiden? From the way he looked at her, Harmony would bet it wasn't just casual friendship.

She joined in the conversation with Trey, Nikki, and Angela for a bit, then Nikki checked her silver-and-rhinestone watch and excused herself. Harmony was certain she was going off to join Jake somewhere, who had disappeared while the women were initiating Aiden into the group.

And so the fun began.

She wondered where the two of them had decided to go . . . what they would do. There was a sweet exhilaration to the first encounter on these vacations. Like having sex for the first time after a long dry spell. It was heady and exciting. Naughty and thrilling.

She was glad Nikki and Angela accepted Aiden and had given him an exciting experience he'd probably never even dreamed of before. She glanced at him and his friend on the dance floor. Did he intend to include this Mia in his fun? Why exactly was she here anyway?

"Would you like to dance again?" Cole offered his hand.

She nodded and followed him to the dance floor.

Aiden slid his arm around Mia. "So where's Craig?"

He couldn't believe he still remembered the guy's name. It seemed odd she'd come on vacation without him.

"We're not together anymore."

"Why are you here, Mia? Did you know I would be here?
This is a hell of a coincidence."

"I don't really want to talk about it here on the dance
floor."

He nodded. He didn't believe for a minute that her being
here was merely a coincidence. Mia hated being without a
man in her life. Could it be that now Craig was history, she
wanted Aiden back?

Was she here to come between Harmony and him? But
that didn't sound like Mia.

The one thing he knew was that she hated to travel alone,
and she wouldn't have come all this way unless it was something really important. Alarm jolted through him. Maybe she
was in some kind of trouble. Maybe she needed his help.

Harmony stepped from the carpet onto the glossy wood
dance floor. As Cole took Harmony's hand and slid his arm
around her waist, she felt a quiver of awareness. He drew her
close and began to move to the music. The heat of his body
so close to hers reminded her of hot, sultry nights in his
arms. Tender caresses, loving looks, heated passion. Her heart
hammered in her chest.

He smiled as he gazed into her eyes while deftly guiding
her around the dance floor.

"So tell me about you and this new man in your life. How
long have you been going out?"

"It's been almost a year now." She understood his curiosity, but she found it difficult to talk to Cole about Aiden.

"Really? So did you know him before the group vacation last year?" He twirled her around, then drew her close again.

"No, I met him a couple of weeks later. Skiing actually."

He smiled. "But you don't ski."

One of the members had suggested a winter vacation at a ski resort one year, possibly Whistler near Vancouver, but Harmony and Nikki both couldn't ski and hadn't wanted to hang out at a snowy resort with nothing to do. Although they could still take part in the more erotic adventures at a ski resort, it wouldn't be the same as the sunny, tropical locales they usually visited. Besides, living in Buffalo, she got quite enough of winter without having to endure it during her vacation. She found a tropical location much more conducive to sexy behavior.

"True, I don't ski, but Leena from work talked me into going with her." She shrugged. "It was just for the day and I figured I really should give it a try. Aiden found me in a pile of skis and limbs so he spent the day teaching me how to ski."

Cole nodded. "And now you're serious enough about him to bring him here." He searched her face.

She nodded. She hadn't been looking forward to telling Cole she might be getting married.

SIX

She tugged her gaze from his and leaned her head against his shoulder.

"So what's the story with this friend of Aiden's? Did he invite her along to even out the group?"

Harmony shook her head. "Not that he told me."

Damn, she shouldn't make it sound like that. Of course he hadn't invited her along. She watched Aiden and Mia glide across the floor, comfortable and familiar with each other.

"I get the impression you're not thrilled with her being here."

Harmony shrugged. "I'm just trying to figure out what she's doing here, that's all. It seems an odd coincidence." She gazed into his eyes and smiled. "But enough about that. How has the year been for you?"

"Good. My business is booming and I moved to Vancouver."

A few years ago, Cole had moved to Canada to start a new business venture. She didn't remember the exact details, but it had something to do with high-tech special effects for movies.

"I bought a condo downtown." He swirled her around to the music. "Mountains on one side, ocean on the other."

"It must be gorgeous. I wish I could see it."

He practically stopped on the dance floor, his hot charcoal gaze searing her . . . then he slowly began to move to the music again.

71

"You know if you ever wanted to, you'd be more than welcome."

"But you know the rules . . ." Harmony reminded him.

When the group had first decided to meet every year, they had agreed that none of them would contact each other during the year—and definitely not visit, except for Trey and Jake, of course, who still lived near the university. The idea was to keep the excitement and, in the long run, to keep the group going. If members started dating outside the group—and ultimately breaking up, or even getting married—it would ruin the group dynamics.

His arm tightened around her waist.

"Harmony, those rules were made twelve years ago. A lot has changed since then."

Her heart thumped louder as she realized what he was saying, but she thought of Aiden and—

"Don't let a silly set of rules stop you," said Cole.

"From what, Cole?" she asked. "Remember Aiden?"

She glanced across the floor. Aiden held Mia close to his body. A little too close for Harmony's comfort. Which on the one hand seemed a little ridiculous given the nature of these vacations. But on the other hand, Harmony was beginning to sense he had a history with this woman.

"Sorry. You're right." Cole smiled and the warmth in his dark eyes melted through her. "But we're here now." He nuzzled her ear and sparks flared down her spine. "So what do you say, dream girl? Want to slip away?"

Temptation sparked at the thought of being in Cole's

arms, feeling his hot hard body pressed against her naked skin, his thick cock pushing into her. It didn't help that she could feel his bulge growing against her stomach.

"No, I don't think so. Aiden—"

"Aiden can join us." He grinned. "Though I'd rather this first time be just the two of us."

An image shimmered through her brain. Of Cole in front of her. Aiden behind her. Their three bodies pressed tight.

She shook her head. "That's not going to happen."

He raised an eyebrow.

"He does know what goes on with the group, doesn't he?"

"Yes, but I think I have to . . . ease him into it."

"Exactly how do you plan to do that?"

"I'm not sure. I've been struggling with that ever since he agreed to come."

When Harmony and Cole returned to the table, Aiden was there but Mia had gone.

Before Harmony had a chance to sit, Aiden stood up and took her hand.

"Would you dance with me?"

She nodded and accompanied him to the floor. His arms encircled her and she snuggled against him. It felt odd going from Cole's arms to Aiden's, but not at all unpleasant.

"So how does it work . . . tonight?" Aiden asked. "How are people going to decide . . . you know, who and where . . . ?"

She glanced up at his face. He seemed preoccupied with something.

"It's pretty casual the first night. However it unfolds."

He nodded. "I was thinking I might just leave you to it. I'd really like to talk to Mia." He tightened his hand around hers and, with a firm hand pressed to her back, negotiated her around a couple leaving the dance floor. "It's not like her to travel alone. I want to make sure everything's okay with her. Find out why she's here."

Harmony raised an eyebrow. "I was wondering about that, too."

She was surprised he was willing to leave her to have sex with other men, while he went in pursuit of an old "friend." Probably an old *girlfriend* from the way he was acting. And that made her wonder.

"How close a friend is she?" Harmony asked. "Did you two—"

"Hey, do you mind if I cut in?" Trey rested his hand on Harmony's shoulder. "After all, you two can be together all the time."

Aiden squeezed Harmony's hand then relinquished it to Trey.

"Be my guest."

Aiden kissed her cheek.

"So I'll see you later," he murmured close to her ear while glancing at the other man. "I assume tomorrow morning."

She nodded, unwilling to tell him not to go. How could

she, when he'd just basically approved of her going off to
have sex with Trey?

This was such a weird situation. She'd known it would be
awkward having Aiden here, but she'd never anticipated
this.

SEVEN

Harmony barely noticed as Trey led her around the dance floor.

"What are you planning to do tonight?" he asked. "I'd love to slip away with you, or join you and Aiden . . . and whoever."

She gazed into his warm brown eyes which were flecked with gold. The soft light glinted from the diamond stud in his ear.

"Aiden and I aren't staying together tonight."

Trey smiled. "Great. I think Angela and Cole are still free. We could do the four of us, or . . ." He grinned and kissed her hand. "Just you and me."

She smiled at him, remembering the feel of his hands on her body and the attentive way he always touched her, but she didn't feel like partying right now and she sure as heck didn't feel like joining in on any sexual activities.

"Actually, I think I'm just going to go back to my room. Alone."

He blinked. "Really? You feeling okay?"

"Yeah, just a little tired."

"Would you just like some company?"

She rested her hand on his cheek. He was actually willing to give up his first night of wild and crazy sex to provide her with platonic companionship.

"That's very sweet, but I wouldn't dream of depriving Angela of your talents."

He smiled and drew her closer, knowing her well enough to recognize when her mind was made up. She rested her head on his shoulder.

When the song ended, Trey accompanied her back to the table. She finished her drink.

"I'm going to call it a night," she said to Cole, Angela, and Trey, the three remaining people at the table.

"You're kidding," Angela exclaimed, grinning. "You're leaving me here with two hunky men all on my own?"

Harmony smiled. "I'm sure you'll figure out something."

Angela rested her hand on Harmony's. "You okay, honey? It's not like you to . . ."

Harmony patted her hand. "I'm fine. There's still the whole vacation ahead of us."

As she stood up, Cole sent her a questioning glance and she smiled. "I'll see you tomorrow."

She wandered across the crowded ballroom feeling a little

lost. Why was she here? Had she just endangered her relationship with Aiden?

Harmony strolled down the escalator to the main level, then crossed the lobby toward the back doors. She stepped onto the stone patio at the back of the hotel and watched the water wash up on the shore, the sound of the rolling waves soothing in the salty night air.

Had Aiden gone off with another woman because he couldn't handle the position she'd put him in? Or did he figure being here meant it was okay to just go off and have sex with any woman he wanted? Including an old girlfriend.

If that's what Mia was.

She sat down at the bar by the pool and ordered a drink. As she watched the moon shimmering on the ocean, a man offered to buy her a drink, but she politely declined. She certainly had enough men to choose from already.

After about an hour, she stood up, signed her check, and headed for the boardwalk along the beach. The warm sultry air filled her lungs with a salty tang as she walked along the wooden deck. She smiled as she glanced at the palm trees beside the walkway, then the glittering ocean to her right. It certainly was a beautiful place.

It was getting late but she couldn't face going to her room alone. Not yet. She made her way back to the hotel and crossed the lobby. Maybe she'd check out the indoor pool and the gym. She opened her small evening bag and tugged out her handy VIP key card. They were closed now, but with this she could get in.

She went down a carpeted hallway to the stairs. Once down a flight she came across a door marked GYM. She slid her card in the slot, waited for the indicator light to glow green, then pulled open the door. There were several large weight machines, a line of treadmills and—

A sound startled her. Someone was here. Actually, probably at least two people, she realized as the nature of the sound became apparent. A woman moaning in pleasure.

She peeked around a corner and saw a man and a woman among the stationary bicycles. It was Nikki and Cole. Nikki was sitting on a recumbent bike, leaning against the backrest with her feet perched on the handlebars while Cole bobbed between her legs. Her fingers curled through his black hair as she moaned.

Nikki had gone off with Jake earlier, or so Harmony had assumed, but a couple of hours had passed since then. Clearly, she'd switched partners.

The sight of Nikki totally naked on the bike, her free hand stroking over her hard nipple, and Cole's head between her legs, sent exciting thrills through Harmony. It was such a sexy sight, and she could just imagine Cole's talented tongue toying with her own clit, then plunging into her wet slit.

Harmony's hand slid to her breast and she stroked herself. She remembered what it felt like to have Cole's face in her pussy. He loved to lick her then nuzzle his tongue inside her opening. Her breasts ached. She pinched her hard, needy nipple.

As Cole stroked Nikki's thigh with one hand, his face

firmly pressed into her dark brown curls, Nikki sucked in a deep breath, then wailed as she came to orgasm.

As Harmony wondered if she should slip away or go out and join them, Cole grasped Nikki around the waist with his big hands and lifted her up, then carried her to a pile of exercise mats, about three feet high, at the side of the room. He sat her on top and she opened her legs, then wrapped one around his thigh as his long, hard cock slid into her.

Harmony pinched her nipple harder, then toyed with the other one. Cole glided forward as he impaled Nikki. She clung to him and he thrust forward and back, forward and back.

"Oh, Cole. Fuck me, baby."

He thrust faster.

Mesmerized, Harmony watched his long purple shaft glide in and out of Nikki's body. She tweaked her nipples harder at the erotic sight.

"Yeah, honey, I'm so close."

Nikki clung to him as he thrust. Deeper and faster.

Harmony tugged her skirt up, her hand diving under the hem, then along her thighs. Heat flushed through her. She could feel her core filling with moisture. Her fingers stroked over the crotch of her panties as Cole fucked Nikki on the mats across the room.

Oh, God, she wanted a man. But not Cole.

Actually, she *did* want Cole. Really, *really* wanted him . . . but she wasn't ready to face the intensity of his touch. And Aiden was off with . . . what's-her-name. Where Trey and Jake were, she didn't know.

She ached with need.

Nikki wailed, then screamed as Cole pounded into her. Harmony teased her clit with her fingertip, vibrating over it. Pressure built within her.

Finally, he slowed and Harmony realized they were almost done. She hesitated, aching for release, but knowing she wasn't close enough. She tugged her hand from between her legs and dropped the hem of her dress, then smoothed down the skirt. She scooted toward the door before they got a chance to see her. Not that they'd mind.

As she hurried down the hall, she saw them through the glass as they entered the pool area from the other side. Naked, they dove into the pool without glancing in her direction. She strode up the stairs, then toward the elevators. One stood open and she stepped inside, then pushed fourteen. She slumped against the back of the elevator, sucking in air and aching for release. She watched the beautiful view of the moonlight on the ocean through the glass as she traveled upward.

Aiden walked into the lounge and past people chatting around tables lit by small candles. Soft music played in the background, but quietly enough to talk over. Not like the noisy ballroom.

He caught sight of Mia sitting at a booth in the back corner. Two drinks sat in front of her. A beer in a frosty pilsner glass and a glass of white wine.

He sat down and sipped the beer she'd ordered for him. He stared at her for a moment and took in the way the soft candlelight glowed on her shiny auburn hair as it cascaded over her shoulders in waves—he remembered the silky feel of it between his fingers—the gentle swell of her breasts, which made his heart thump a little faster, and her deep-sea blue eyes, full of emotion.

"So why did you fly all the way down here, Mia?" he began. Why waste time with a long preamble?

She folded her hands in front of her.

"Right to the point as always." She sipped her wine. "I came here to see you."

His eyebrow arched. "Why? You could have waited until I got back next week. After all, I only live across the city."

She toyed with the stem of her glass.

"Next week would have been too late."

"What's wrong, Mia? Are you sick?"

She shook her head. "Only about the fact that I let you go." Her gaze met his and the intensity shocked him. "I was an idiot to run off on you. I loved you. I still do."

Her words slammed him in the gut. She loved him?

He leaned back in his chair. "You sure had a weird way of showing it. Telling me you'd answer my proposal later. Ignoring my calls. Then running off with another guy."

"I know. I kick myself every day. I just . . ." Her mouth compressed and her hands curled into fists. "I was scared. I didn't believe I deserved you."

He took a swig of his drink. She placed her warm, delicate

hand on his, but he drew it away. She wrapped her fingers around her glass. "You were wonderful and loving and . . . everything a woman could want. I was just afraid I wouldn't live up to your expectations. I was afraid you'd fall out of love with me and . . . that would hurt too much."

"So you figured you'd hurt me instead."

She rested her hand on his wrist.

"I'm really, really sorry."

This time he didn't pull away. Tears shimmered in her eyes and Aiden felt like a heel. He knew she had self-esteem issues. Her father had done a number on her as a kid, making her feel worthless and stupid, even though she'd aced school and went on to earn a degree in biology and now worked as a lab technician. It didn't matter. She still believed she was the stupid, worthless girl her father had always accused her of being. Unlovable and unworthy.

"How did you know where I was?" he asked.

"Cindy."

Of course. His very helpful sister. He never should have told Cindy he was going to ask Harmony to marry him, but he'd been excited. And he'd really thought she'd say yes. Not pull a Mia on him.

No, he wouldn't think like that. Harmony had asked him to wait for an answer, but she'd invited him on this trip with her. Trusted him with her secret.

Cindy, on the other hand, wanted him to marry Mia. That's why she'd introduced them in the first place. Clearly, that's why she was interfering now.

"Cindy told you that I proposed to Harmony, I take it."

Mia nodded. "And that she won't answer you until the end of the week."

She took his hands in hers, her warm, delicate fingers curling around his.

"I love you, Aiden, and I'd like to finally give you my answer."

God damn it. Why did life have to be so complicated? Why couldn't she have just said yes when he'd asked her over a year ago?

When the elevator stopped, Harmony tugged her key card out of her evening bag, then exited the elevator and walked down the hall. She was still hot and hungry after watching Cole and Nikki in the gym. She slipped the card in the door and when the light turned green, she turned the knob and pushed it open.

Would Aiden be inside waiting for her? Probably not. Even if he wasn't with that Mia woman, he would have gone back to his own room. She closed the door behind her as she peered into her room, hoping she might find him waiting for her despite her thoughts to the contrary.

She stepped past the bathroom and glanced at the bed, then the sitting room beyond. No Aiden. She walked over to the door to the adjoining room.

Should she knock? Should she just go inside?

She leaned against the door and listened. She could hear

some kind of sound. Was he in there watching TV? She smiled. He had a habit of falling asleep when he watched TV. She tapped lightly and waited, but he didn't answer. She turned the knob—still unlocked—and pushed the door open a crack.

And froze.

She saw two figures on the bed, obviously making love. Anger surged through her at the thought that Aiden was in there with his ex-girlfriend. She shoved the door all the way open and marched inside.

Wait, there were more than two people. As her eyes got used to the dim light she realized there were three figures on the bed. Two male and one female.

And neither of the males was Aiden.

Angela was on her side with one leg curled around Jake's thigh while he moved forward and back. Some of his hair had pulled free from the elastic and wisped across his face. Behind Jake, Trey was stroking her breasts while caressing Jake's ass as he watched Jake making love to her, engrossed by Jake's cock sliding in and out.

The ache in Harmony's body intensified. Her hand slipped to her breast again and she stroked her tight, hard nipple. Excitement flared inside her. She watched for a few moments, then stepped farther into the room.

"Harmony," Trey said. "Come join us."

She reached behind and unzipped her dress, then let it fall to the floor.

"Why are you in here?" she asked as she kicked off her shoes.

Trey grinned and sat up on the bed while the other two kept at it.

"Here, let me help you," he offered as she reached around to unfasten her bra. She stepped toward him. "It was Angela's idea. She suggested we come see if you and Aiden wanted to play. When we didn't find either of you here, she thought if we started up in here and Aiden walked in on us, he might decide to join in."

He reached around her and unfastened the three hooks on the back of her black bra, then drew it away. The brush of Trey's fingers on her skin made her pulse race. He stroked her breasts and she sucked in a deep breath.

"You have such beautiful breasts. Have I ever told you that before?"

"About a hundred times." Harmony smiled and curled her arms around his neck. "But I never get tired of hearing it."

Harmony nipped his ear, dragging her tongue over his diamond stud. He grinned and leaned forward to take one bead-like nipple in his mouth. The feel of him sucking on it made her knees weak. She leaned against him and he wrapped his hands around her, pressing her belly to his chest as he sucked on one nipple, then the other.

Behind him, Angela moaned in orgasm and Jake grunted as they undulated in a spectacular climax. Trey continued to suck Harmony's nipple as his hands strayed over her buttocks, left bare by her lacy thong. A few moments later, she felt another pair of hands on her ass, then a warm mouth pressing light kisses down her spine. Jake. She opened her eyes, which had drifted closed under Trey's attention, to see Angela sitting beside Trey. Angela watched as Trey sucked on Harmony's breast, stroking her own nipples to hard pebbles. Jake began to roll Harmony's thong down.

Trey continued to lick and suck her nipples, while Jake drew the panties over Harmony's feet then tossed them aside. Angela plumped a pillow and leaned back against it, then stroked between her legs while she watched the two men pleasure Harmony.

Jake nuzzled Harmony's ear from behind. "Harmony, spread your legs."

Harmony did as he asked and Jake crouched down, then kissed Harmony's calves. Trey's tongue twirled around her nipple, while he pinched the other one between his fingertips. Wild, wonderful sensations careened through her from every direction.

Jake continued up her thighs, sending goose bumps along her skin. Trey eased her back and shifted from the bed to his knees as he kissed down her ribs, to her stomach, then dabbed his tongue into her naval. She laughed as she raked her fingers through his tousled blond hair. Excitement swirled through her as he continued downward to her waxed pussy, then eased her legs apart more and kissed her folds.

Behind her, Jake laid light kisses along her buttocks, while he stroked between her cheeks. Trey licked her pussy as Jake pressed his fingertip to her back opening and stroked. His other hand glided between her legs and over her pussy, as Trey shifted to her clit. She moaned and clutched Trey's head to her as his tongue teased and cajoled her sensitive bud. Jake dipped his finger inside her, then stroked back to her ass and twirled over her opening.

"You guys are doing a great job," Angela said, her finger flicking over her clit.

She pushed herself from the bed and insinuated herself between Harmony's feet, then took Trey's cock into her mouth. He mumbled something appreciative against Harmony's throbbing clit. Jake's slippery finger pushed against her ass, then slid inside her opening. She threw her head back and wailed.

"Oh, yes." It had been a year since she'd had action back there. And it had been Jake then, too.

Jake slid another finger inside her. Trey slid a finger into her wet slit and stroked her opening, sending vibrant bursts of pleasure through her. Angela's head bobbed up and down on Trey. He clamped his hand over her head, then stroked her hair back.

"Angie, I can't handle any more."

She shifted away, then sat on the bed with a huge grin on her face.

"Well, I wouldn't want to deprive Harmony of that beautiful cock in full bloom," she said, then began to stroke her slit again.

Trey reached between Harmony's knees and grasped Jake's cock and pumped it while Jake slipped a third finger inside Harmony's rear opening, stretching it. *Getting it ready for his long, slender cock.* Always perfect for just that purpose.

Trey covered her with his mouth again. She sucked in air as her insides throbbed with need. After a minute of Trey's clever tongue bouncing and swirling on her sensitive bud, while Jake continued to swirl his fingers inside her, Harmony was way past ready.

"Will somebody please get up here and fuck me already?"

"Well, there's an invitation I can't pass up," Trey said.

He stood up then sat on the edge of the bed. He took her hand and drew her forward. Jake's fingers slipped free and he followed them. Trey's erect penis curved upward, calling to her.

Harmony reached back and wrapped her hand around Jake's cock as she watched Trey stroke up and down his long shaft. She tugged on Jake until he eased closer then she crouched down and pulled his cock to her lips. Angela slid behind him and massaged his balls, while Harmony ran her tongue the length of his shaft. She wrapped her lips around Jake's cock-head and sucked gently while Trey stroked his curved cock and watched in fascination.

"You look a little distracted there," Trey said. "Didn't you just ask me to . . . what was it you wanted me to do now?"

Harmony sucked hard on Jake's cock, then released it and stood up, grinning at Trey.

"Just fuck me, will you?"

"Ah, that was it."

She straddled him. He guided her hips forward until she was poised over his cock, then he drove forward, impaling her with one sure thrust.

"Oh, God, yes."

His long, wide cock stretched her. He smiled and pulled back slowly, then thrust forward again, stroking her sensitive canal. Her hands slid around his back, her nails digging into his flesh as she drew him toward her. She squeezed her intimate muscles around him.

"Hey, don't forget about me," Jake said.

Trey lay back on the bed and she leaned forward, on her hands and knees above him, presenting her ass to Jake.

Angela grabbed a tube from the bedside table and tossed it to Jake. A moment later, his slick cock pressed against Harmony's opening. Trey licked one of her nipples while Jake pressed into her slowly. She pushed her muscles outward to ease him in, then his cock-head slipped inside, stretching her in a pleasurably painful way. His hands cupped her hips and he pushed his shaft in deeper. And deeper.

Now they were both inside her. She sighed, loving this feeling of being pressed between two men who desired her.

Jake drew out a little, then eased forward again, then held her tight to his pelvis. Trey thrust inside her, then thrust again, then again, each time pushing her back against Jake, driving Jake's cock deeper into her. A wave of pleasure swelled through her, rising to a feverish level.

The three of them moved together. Two cocks inside her. Deepening her pleasure with each stroke.

"Harmony, honey." Trey's cock swelled. "I'm close."

"Me, too," Jake said.

She nodded. So was she. Her whole body seemed to quiver

in anticipation. Both Trey and Jake stiffened at the same time and Jake groaned. Both cocks erupted into her with liquid heat and pleasure exploded through her body.

Her wail could have shattered the windows with its intensity. She shot into a free-floating bliss that numbed her mind as her body soared on a sea of pure ecstasy.

As she floated back to earth, she became vaguely aware of her surroundings. She shoved her hair back from her face and smiled up at Trey. Jake nuzzled her neck and she leaned her head back against his shoulder, lingering in the blissful afterglow.

A movement across the room drew her attention and she gazed over lazily. Then her breath caught.

Aiden stood inside the doorway, a stormy expression on his face.

EIGHT

When Aiden had pushed open the door to his room, he'd been shocked by the sight of several naked people entwined on his bed. Two men—Trey and Jake—were making love to a woman. Then his gaze caught on the woman's face.

Harmony.

Her hair flowed in shiny black waves over her face as she arched over Trey and moaned as Jake's long, slender cock drove into her from behind.

God, what a sexy sight. She was so uninhibited. So wildly passionate. Aiden's cock had pushed to attention as she'd wailed in climax. He'd ached to drive his cock into her, just as Trey and Jake had been doing.

Now she stared at him with wide, uncertain eyes.

Jake stepped back and helped Harmony to her feet.

Aiden stalked toward her, his gaze fixed on her soft, full lips. Trey pushed himself to his feet and helped the others gather clothes that had been strewn around the room while

Harmony continued to stare at Aiden, her hair in wild disarray around her face.

Harmony watched as Aiden strode closer, tensing as she waited for his jealous tirade. Regret washed through her as she realized she never should have brought him here. What did he think of her now?

Aiden stood beside the bed, staring at her, his hands clenched at his sides, his breathing heavy.

"I guess we should leave you two alone," Trey said, then gave her a peck on the cheek.

He and the others dressed quickly.

"See you tomorrow," Angela said as Trey pulled open the door. Harmony just nodded, her gaze never leaving Aiden's.

"Aiden," she started as soon as the door closed behind them, "I . . ."

"God, Harmony."

She felt tears well up. Oh, God, he hated her. "I'm sorry, I never should have—"

But he flung off his shirt, then dropped his pants to the floor. As soon as he peeled off his boxers, she saw his cock standing tall and proud.

"I want you so much." He kissed her with intense passion, his lips moving on hers, his tongue driving into her mouth in an insistent but tender invasion. He sucked her tongue as he eased her onto the bed, then prowled over her. His cock slid along her thighs. She grabbed him and guided him to her opening. He drove inside in a single stroke.

"Oh, yes, Aiden. Yes."

He drew back and drove into her hard and deep. She gasped. His hot, hard cock speared into her again and again, driving her need higher and higher. Blinding bliss spiked through her and she wailed in a joyful orgasm. Aiden tensed and groaned as he joined her in climax.

Harmony awoke to the feel of something tickling her nose. She opened her eyes to see the dark, tanned skin of Aiden's chest and the light smattering of dark, curly hair that teased her nose. Aiden's warm arms encircled her, holding her tightly to his body, and she felt safe and cozy.

Bright sunshine lit the room and she knew this was going to be a fabulous day. She turned her head and kissed his neck.

"Good morning," he said in a raspy, morning voice.

"Mmm, it certainly is." She kissed his chest, luxuriating in the feel of his warm skin under her lips.

He stroked her hair as she licked his tight nipple.

"As much as I love what you're doing, I feel I should point out that we're going to miss breakfast . . . and I know how much you love breakfast."

She glanced at the clock. Ten seventeen. The restaurant would stop serving breakfast at eleven.

He was right. She did love breakfast. Especially when someone else made it.

If she rushed, she could probably take her shower, get dressed, and make it to the restaurant in time to order breakfast with a few minutes to spare.

On the other hand . . . She stroked her hand down his stomach, over the well-defined abs. She felt his cock stir against her and her insides ached. There were other things she loved even better.

She slid downward and teased the tip of his delicious member with her tongue.

"I'll make you a deal." She licked him again, then circled her hands around his shaft. "We'll spend another ten minutes in bed, then you go down and order me breakfast while I finish getting ready."

She knew Aiden could shower and dress in fifteen minutes. She swallowed his cock-head into her mouth, circling her tongue around and around his sensitive flesh.

"That is so absolutely . . ." He groaned. ". . . a deal."

Aiden stepped outside into the fresh, warm breeze and the sound of the ocean caressing the shore. He breathed in the morning air and smiled.

Paradise.

The hostess led him across the stone patio to a cozy, round table near the low wall of raised planters filled with colorful tropical plants that bordered the edge of the outdoor restaurant. He gazed past the exotic red blossoms to the stunning view of the turquoise ocean below. Off to the right, stone stairs led to lower patio levels with similar walls all the way to the beach about twenty yards below.

He sat down and watched a couple on the beach race into

the sparkling surf, waiting for Harmony to finish her shower and meet him at the restaurant. The hostess set two menus on the table and called a waitress over to pour him a cup of coffee. When she arrived, he ordered breakfast right away, then sat back to enjoy his coffee.

"May I join you?"

He glanced up to see Mia standing across from him, her hand poised on the back of the chair. The sun glistened on her long, auburn hair.

She wore a white sundress that fit snugly over her breasts then flared to a wide skirt that fluttered in the soft breeze, revealing occasional glimpses of her slender thighs. He hesitated, and she used the opportunity to draw the chair closer to him and sit down.

"I just wanted to let you know I meant what I said last night."

"Mia, I told you . . . I'm in love with Harmony. I've asked her to marry me."

"And she hasn't answered you yet." She reached across the table and took his hand, gazing at him with big blue eyes. "You know what my answer would be."

He drew his hand from her grasp. "Now, but what about when I asked you last time?"

"I was confused. I didn't know what I really wanted, and I've regretted it every day since. I've done a lot of soul searching since then and now—"

"Now I know what I really want, and that's Harmony." At the stricken look in her eye, he took her hand again. "I'm sorry, Mia. I don't mean to hurt you, but I love Harmony. And you . . . I think you're just feeling off balance. You're looking to me because you feel safe with me. I'll admit that we had a lot of good times—"

Her fingers tightened around his. "No, Aiden." She shook her head. "I really love you."

"Mia . . ."

"I know. It stinks that I'm coming and saying this now—I know how crazy it must seem, but if I didn't tell you . . . if I didn't even try . . . then I would always regret it. I'd have to live every single day knowing I'd missed my chance at real happiness." She squeezed his hand. "Aiden, don't you think if Harmony really loved you . . . she wouldn't hold you off for an answer? If she *really* loved you, wouldn't she fling herself into your arms and . . . ?"

"That's exactly what *you* did—held me off for an answer."

"Yes, but that's because I wasn't sure of my feelings. I'll admit it, I freaked out, but losing you made me realize how much baggage I was carrying around, and now I know what a fool I was. Listen, Aiden, the last thing I want to do is come in here and mess up your new relationship, but when your sister told me that Harmony didn't accept your proposal, I just hoped it was a sign that you and I were meant to be together—and I had to come here."

"If the answer's the right one, it'll be the same, a week later, or a year."

Uncertainty crawled through him. If Harmony really did

love him, why hadn't she said yes right away? And if he were to believe Mia loved him, which woman would he truly want to spend his life with?

He knew Mia. She wasn't a manipulative person. She truly believed she loved him. And maybe she did. An ache washed through him. He'd loved her so long . . .

But he had Harmony now. And Mia had no one. She was probably just mistaking her loneliness for loving him. He reached across the table and ran his finger along her soft cheek in a gentle stroke.

"Don't worry, Mia. You'll find someone."

"Aiden?"

He glanced around to see Harmony watching them, her sharp green gaze fixed on their linked hands, then the soft, dewy look of Mia's sea blue eyes.

The moment Harmony had stepped into the terrace restaurant, spotted Aiden at the table and realized the cozy couple staring into each other's eyes like two devoted lovers were Aiden and his so-called friend, her stomach had clenched as though clutched in an iron fist. For a moment, she'd just stared, then Aiden had stroked the woman's cheek, tenderly and with a gentleness in his eyes that tore through Harmony. Denial washed through her, but she could not ignore the damning evidence in front of her.

Even now, as the two of them stared at her, their hands remained entwined. The other woman glanced at her and had the grace to look guilty. She released Aiden's hand.

"I'll . . . uh . . . let you two get to your breakfast," Mia said as she grabbed her purse from the ground beside her chair and pushed herself to her feet. Her back stiff, she turned and strolled away, across the patio, then ascended the stairs to the hotel.

Harmony stared at Aiden. "You two looked pretty cozy."

Aiden dragged his gaze from Mia as she disappeared into the hotel and refocused on Harmony.

"It's not what you think."

Anger flared through her and her hands balled into fists by her side.

What kind of fool did he think she was? The two of them had been sitting there, right out in the open, holding hands, acting all lovey-dovey. She'd seen them. Every other person on the terrace had seen them.

"Then what the hell was it?"

Aiden's back stiffened. "Mia is a friend. She's going through a tough time right now."

"Don't tell me. She's just broken up with someone . . . and she flew all the way here to tell you about it."

"I know it seems like a coincidence that she's here—"

"You think?" She crossed her arms. "*Is* it a coincidence?"

He sucked in a deep breath and sighed. "Harmony, please sit down."

She glanced around and realized people were staring at her. She moved to the chair across from him and sank into it. It was still warm from the other woman's presence.

Her heart sank.

Just when Harmony had started to believe that Aiden accepted her for who she was . . .

"She's an old girlfriend, isn't she?"

His mouth compressed into a thin line. He met her gaze and nodded.

"How serious was your relationship with her?"

"Pretty serious."

Her chest tightened as she remembered one time when they'd visited his sister, Cindy, and she'd told Harmony that Aiden had been essentially engaged about eight months before he'd met her. What had she said that woman's name was? Melody? Or Marion? Or . . .

"She's the one you asked to marry you, isn't she?"

His eyebrows compressed together. "How do you know about . . . ?" He sighed. "Cindy."

She nodded. Oh, God. It *was* her. Harmony's fingers tapped nervously on the empty cup in front of her.

"Mia broke up with the guy she'd been dating," Aiden said. "Cindy told her where to find me. But Harmony—"

"I don't need to hear any more. I understand perfectly."

Aiden watched a mix of emotions flutter through Harmony's eyes. He didn't know what to say to assure her. He didn't like her confrontational manner, but he reeled in his impatience. Being faced with a fiancé's old flame would throw anyone off kilter. Not that he was Harmony's fiancé . . . yet.

"Did you sleep with her last night?" Harmony demanded.

Her words stung. He had done everything right. Last night, faced with the woman he had once been in love with, a woman he'd been sure was his soul mate, he had faced down temptation and chosen Harmony. Yet here she sat, accusing him unjustly.

"Last night, you had sex with two men right in front of me. What right do you have to be angry at me?"

Her eyes widened. He pushed himself to his feet and strode away, trying to ignore her stricken expression.

NINE

Harmony watched Aiden leave. There was an ache in her chest and it was difficult to breathe. His words rang harshly inside her head.

You're a slut. A whore who fucks men in front of me. Who the hell are you to tell me who I can and can't fuck?

Those might not have been his exact words, but that's what he'd meant. At least he hadn't hit her. When Lance had reacted after that night with him and his roommate . . .

His exact words remained etched on her brain.

You fucking whore. He'd backed her against the wall with flames searing from his eyes. *What was with the fucking gang bang with me and my roommate last night?* He'd leaned toward her with a cruel leer. *I thought you were a normal woman. Not a slut.*

He'd smacked her across the face and physically dragged her across the room, then shoved her out the door. Her arm had bashed against the door frame as he'd pushed her out, leaving a nasty bruise, and she'd landed on her ass in the hallway. He'd slammed the door in her face.

She shuddered at the intense memory. It could have been worse. Her head had barely missed smashing against a heavy oak table in the apartment hallway.

She dashed away tears as she sucked in a deep, quivering breath. Just like Lance, Aiden had enjoyed himself last night. He'd watched her, getting excited by the sight of her with Trey and Jake and Angela, then he had taken her with a passionate lust. As always, though, at the dawn of a new day, a man could find a new perspective on things.

Except Jake, and Trey and Cole. With them, she could be herself. They loved her for who she was.

"Hey there. How's it going?"

Cole, dressed in a soft beige shirt and dark khaki shorts, sat down across from her. The breeze caught his hair and a wavy black lock swept over his forehead. His full lips were turned up in a smile, but as soon as she lifted her face and gazed at him, his smile ebbed and concern darkened his gray eyes.

"What's wrong, dream girl?"

She pushed aside thoughts of Lance and his cruel treatment. *That was then and this is now.*

"I had a fight with Aiden. He . . ." Her throat constricted.

"Is it about his friend . . . Mia?" Cole asked.

She nodded. That's what had started it all. "She's not just a friend," Harmony explained. "Not even just an ex-girlfriend." She fiddled with the spoon lying next to the empty mug on the pristine white tablecloth. "He wanted to marry her."

Cole whistled. "So she's here to pick up where they left off?"

"That's right."

"Did he tell you that?"

She pursed her lips. "He didn't deny it."

He nodded and placed his hand over hers. The feel of his big, warm hand enveloping hers was comforting.

"Is it over between the two of you?"

"I hope not . . ." She sucked in a breath, trying to calm herself. ". . . but he stormed away and . . ." Tears overcame her.

Cole pulled his chair closer to hers and stroked her hair. Damn it, he hated to see her like this. Hurt and vulnerable.

"I . . ." She sniffed and picked up the paper napkin from under the fork and blew her nose. "I didn't tell you yesterday that . . ." She blew her nose again. "Aiden proposed to me. Two weeks ago."

"So he's your fiancé?"

"Not exactly. I haven't answered him yet. I told him I wouldn't answer him until after the vacation."

He took her hand and gave it a quick kiss, then grinned.

"I assume that was because you wanted to break it to *me* before you accepted. After all, you did agree to marry me."

It had been a joke they'd had in college—a promise that if neither of them was married by the time they were forty, they'd marry each other.

He sighed for effect.

"Ah, well, since you've clearly chosen another guy over me, maybe I could help you out by seducing this Mia woman away from him. Making love to another beautiful woman is a tough job, I know, but I'm willing to do it for you."

Her lips curled up in a smile at his joking tone. "Are you still trying to pay me back for that time I distracted Bill Walker at the Halloween party so you could put the moves on Tiffany Meyers?" She grinned. "I still remember how your eyes bugged out when you saw her in that tiny cat costume."

He grinned. "Nice try, but we both know you went after Bill for your own reasons. And for the record, I don't need any help attracting the ladies."

"Well, that's true. If you decide to go after Mia, she won't stand a chance."

Her smile faded and she stared down at her hands. She obviously loved this guy Aiden.

"Harmony, why did you wait to accept Aiden's proposal?"

"Because . . . I . . ." She sighed. "I don't let people see this side of me in my regular life. The open, uninhibited side. At least, not anymore."

His teeth clenched together. He could sense an incredible amount of pain hidden behind those words. Someone had hurt her. Badly.

"I wanted him to see me here . . . the way I am. To know that . . ." Her voice cracked and she took a deep breath. "That he'll accept me . . ."

He squeezed her hand.

"Dream girl, any guy who doesn't love you for exactly

who you are doesn't deserve you. Don't let anyone, Aiden or the creep who obviously hurt you . . ."

Her gaze darted to his eyes at his words.

". . . make you think less of yourself." He drew her hand to his mouth and kissed it tenderly. "You are a vital, sexy, wonderful woman. Don't ever forget that."

Harmony let the sound of the waves soothe her as the hot sun warmed her bare skin. A clear blue sky stretched overhead and white sand surrounded them. She pushed her straw hat back and rolled onto her side on the cushioned lounge chair and watched Cole's chest rise and fall. She couldn't tell if he was awake or asleep behind the dark sunglasses he wore. She stroked a finger down his chest, through the curly hairs in the center, over his stomach, then dabbed at his belly button.

"Yes?" He stretched the word out in a long lazy question.

She grinned as he turned his head toward her.

Cole was such a sweetheart. He'd noticed that she'd had her beach bag with her at the table and had suggested she join him for a swim in the ocean. Shortly after they'd returned to their chairs and dried off, a waiter had appeared with a picnic basket and set out a blanket. They'd feasted on egg and bacon sandwiches, a thermos of coffee, and fresh fruit. She'd missed breakfast and he'd known it, so he'd arranged one for her. Typical thoughtful Cole.

He had done everything he could to take her mind off her problems with Aiden and it had almost worked.

"We've been out in the sun a while now and even with a forty-five sunscreen, I think we'd better head back," she suggested.

He quirked up an eyebrow. "You really want to go back?"

It was common sense, but she really didn't want to go. The water and the fresh air soothed her soul.

"Well . . ."

"If it's just the sun you want to get away from, I know this great little place . . . secluded . . . with a waterfall."

"Really?"

He stood up and offered his hand. She took it and pulled herself to her feet, then grabbed her beach bag, stepped into her sandals, and followed him across the fine white sand. He led her to where the beach met wild foliage, then along a path that wound through tall trees. As soon as they stepped into the shade, her skin cooled. They hadn't gone very far when she heard the sound of rushing water. A moment later, they stepped past some large-leafed bushes and before her was a gorgeous waterfall, about twenty feet high, pouring over a craggy rock wall into an emerald pool below.

Cole took her hand and led her to the water's edge.

"It's safe to swim here," he assured.

She grinned wickedly and unfastened her bathing suit top, then dropped it to the grassy earth beneath her feet.

"Ah, it's going to be like that, is it?" He dropped his trunks to the ground.

His cock, semierect, seemed to inflate as she toyed with her skimpy, floral bikini bottom. She dipped her fingers under the front, her pubic curls tickling her fingertips, then she ran them toward her hips, watching his cock rise as his gaze followed the movement of her fingers. She tugged the elastic and shimmied out of her bottoms, dropping them to her ankles. She kicked off her sandals and stepped out of her suit bottoms. Her toes curled into the cool grass beneath her feet.

Standing there staring at him totally naked felt devilishly wicked. He stepped toward her and she smiled, then giggled and dove into the water. He dove in after her.

The water was cool and refreshing against her skin. She swam to the foot of the waterfall and grabbed the deep ledge formed by large, flat rocks behind it and enjoyed the invigorating feel of the cool water splashing over her hair and face.

Cole pulled himself onto the ledge, then grasped her hand and pulled her out of the water and right into his arms. Her breasts pressed tight against his solid chest as his arms tightened around her and his mouth took hers in a passionate assault.

She melted against him, her body thrumming with need. Water poured over one side of her body and he eased them closer to the rock wall, until they were totally behind the waterfall. The world became a blurry haze behind the curtain of water.

"Cole, it's absolutely beautiful here."

He stroked wet strands of hair from her face and tucked them behind her ear with aching tenderness.

"Yes, it is. Almost as beautiful as you."

It might be a corny line, and cliché as all get out, but it still turned her heart to mush. She leaned toward him and offered her mouth again, which he immediately captured. His cool, wet lips felt good on hers. She nuzzled her tongue past them and swirled inside his mouth, tangling with his tongue in a passionate dance.

His hand traveled over her hip, up her ribs, then glided over the side of her breast. She shifted back a little to give him access and almost gasped as his warm hand covered her cool, needy flesh. Her nipple, standing at full attention, pressed into his palm. He stroked, then leaned down and lapped at the nub with his tongue. When he tugged it into the heat of his mouth, she did gasp. Her other nipple wanted . . . Ah, his thumb strummed over it and it ached with pleasure.

Her hand found its way down his stomach and her fingers wrapped around his hot, hard cock. He lapped at her other nipple as she stroked up and down his shaft, which felt like kid leather stretched over hot iron. His hands wrapped around her waist as his mouth worked on one nipple, then the other until she was panting for air. She leaned her head back, into the stream of water, and opened her mouth, then she leaned forward and knelt in front of him. She sucked the tip of his cock into her water-filled mouth, surrounding him in cool water.

"Oh, sweetie."

The warmth of her mouth heated the water . . . and him. She released the water and licked his cock from base to tip, then swallowed it whole. She opened her throat, taking him deep, then she sucked and squeezed.

"Oh, yeah. Oh, sweetheart." His fingers ran through her hair as she bobbed up and down on his delicious cock.

Her free hand stroked his balls, then slid over his rock-hard ass, pulling him closer to her.

"Sweetie . . . I'm really close. . . ."

She sucked harder and he tensed, then hot liquid pulsed into her mouth.

He knelt down beside her and eased her down until she was stretched out on the ledge, one leg flung over the edge, water streaming over it. Cole leaned forward and dipped his tongue into her hot, wet slit. He licked her length, then nuzzled her clit with the very tip of his tongue. Then he licked her again, this time ending with a tiny spiral over her clit.

As the water washed over her leg and his hands swirled over her body—the peaks of her breasts, the plane of her stomach, the curve of her hips, then back to her breasts—heat built within her, pulsing and bubbling. He sucked on her clit and pleasure sparked, then flared white hot.

She clung to his head.

"Yes. That's it."

His finger slipped inside her as he tugged and sucked on her clit. An orgasm washed over her like a tidal wave. She sucked in air, then expelled it in a long, lingering moan.

As she lay there, the water streaming down beside her, the fragrant flowers filling the air with sweetness, she opened her arms to Cole. He prowled over her and kissed her. His hard cock brushed her thigh and she wanted it inside her. She grasped him and tugged, but he laughed.

"Sweetheart, I'm not sure this will work here. There's not much room."

The way the ledge of rocks narrowed in places, it would be dodgy to find a stable position, but she pulled him forward and pressed his cock to her slit. He pushed forward, but at his first solid thrust, his knee slipped and he tumbled sideways into the water, taking her with him. She sucked in a lungful of air as the cool water surrounded her, before she plummeted below the surface. She felt his strong arms grasp her and pull her toward him. As soon as her face broke the surface of the water, she sucked in air, then broke out laughing. His laughter echoed hers as he pulled her against him with one arm while his other hand grasped the rock ledge, then he kissed her soundly.

She glanced around the tranquil clearing and on the opposite side of the pool from where her bag and their bathing suits lay abandoned, she noticed a large rock just the perfect height to sit on.

"Let's go over there," she suggested.

She pushed away from the ledge and swam toward the shore, Cole right behind her. She stepped out of the water to a narrow strip of sand, maybe two yards at its widest, and about three times that long, hugging the shore of the water.

The warm, fine sand squished between her toes. She grabbed Cole's hand and raced toward the rock, laughing. She felt so carefree and happy.

Cole sat down and pulled her onto his lap, his mouth hungrily exploring hers. His cock, wilted from the shock of the cool water, stiffened against her thigh. She thrust her tongue into his mouth and pulsed in and out, just as she longed for his cock to do to her. She drew her mouth away and grinned at him as she slid down his body.

"This guy needs a little coaxing," she said as she wrapped her fingers around his semierect cock.

She licked the head, swirling her tongue around and around the crown, then curled under the ridge. She dove down on him, swallowing him to the hilt and sucked.

He swelled in her mouth until he was fully erect and ready to go. She released him and grinned broadly. She stood up and moved into his arms, but he spun her around.

"It would be a shame to miss this beautiful view," he said as he guided her backward.

He slid his hand to the middle of her back and pressed down, angling her forward. She felt his cock press against her slit from behind, then it glided into her as he eased her onto his lap, his big, thick cock stretching her. At the heady feeling of fullness, she squeezed him tight within her.

"Oh, dream girl. Do that again." As his hands cupped her breasts, she complied with his request, squeezing him mercilessly within her. He groaned.

A snapping sound grabbed her attention and she glanced

across the pool, but lost focus when Cole teased her nipples with his fingertips. Hot sensations rushed from her nipples to her vagina, colliding with the intense pleasure already pulsing there.

She shifted a little on Cole's lap and his cock shifted inside her in an erotic caress. A flash of color in the foliage snagged her attention, but Cole wrapped his hands around her waist and lifted her up, then down, drawing his cock out a little, then driving it inside again. She pushed herself up and down, with the help of his hands to keep her balanced, and threw her head back and moaned at the exquisite pleasure of his wide, hard cock stroking her inner walls.

She felt as if she were being watched and her gaze swept across the opposite bank. Was someone over there? Watching her? Watching Cole drive his cock into her? Heat flushed through her at the idea.

TEN

Harmony's hands slipped to her breasts and she plucked at the nipples, torturing them until the aureoles were hard and pebbled and the tips ached. She shifted downward on Cole and ground against him, driving his cock deep inside her. She stayed motionless like that, pulsing her internal muscles around him.

As she gazed around at the surrounding foliage, hoping to glimpse someone, she licked her lips and smiled invitingly at whoever might be watching, then sucked her fingers into her mouth and stroked them over her nipple.

She pressed her head back against Cole, then nuzzled his neck.

"I think someone's watching us," she said, loud enough for someone across the small pond to hear.

"Really?" He nuzzled her neck and slid one hand up to toy with her other nipple. "They should come out where they can get a better look."

They. So Cole had seen them or at least heard what she had.

The foliage rustled and a man with shoulder-length, wavy dark brown hair stepped into the clearing, followed by another with short, spiky hair, also brown but tinged with strands of caramel. They both looked to be in their mid- to late twenties and both were very good-looking.

They grinned sheepishly.

She smiled back at them as she stroked her hands over Cole's and slid her fingers between his, then guided them upward and cupped her breasts with their entwined hands. Their guests watched with avid interest and one slipped his erection from his navy trunks and began stroking it. At his friend's boldness, the other fellow did the same.

Cole slid his hand downward, sliding free of her fingers, and stroked under her breasts, then lifted them, thrusting them toward the other men.

The sight of their hungry gazes turned her on immensely. She stroked the tips of her nipples as she imagined the men touching her, caressing her.

"Why don't you two come over here and join us?" She sent them her most seductive smile.

As soon as the words were out of her mouth, the bolder of the two dove into the water and swam toward them. Wide-eyed, his friend hesitated. Harmony laughed.

"Wait. There are some condoms in my bag there. In the zippered pouch on the side."

He tugged open the zipper, pulled out the sealed bag with

a half dozen condoms she kept for emergencies, then stuffed it in his pocket and dove into the water. She knew everyone in the group was safe—they always got tested before their annual trip—but she didn't know about these guys. Within moments, the two men stood in front of her, dripping wet.

Both men were fit and muscular, with handsome faces. The bolder one with the shoulder-length hair had a friendly glint in his sky blue eyes, while the other had a lopsided grin that lit up his golden-speckled, green eyes.

She held out her hand to the latter and he stepped toward her, with a quick sidelong glance at his friend. She drew his hand to her breast. His skin was cool from the water, which caused her nipple to ache as it peaked against his palm. As she suspected he would, the other man, needing no invitation now that he understood the rules, stepped forward and grasped her other breast.

She stroked her hand down Green-Eyes' solid chest, then over the bulge in the front of his brown-and-white striped trunks. He pulled out the bag of condoms from his suit, then stepped out of his trunks. She grasped his broad, slightly curved cock. Blue-Eyes, now naked, too, stepped to her other side. He leaned in and sucked her nipple into his mouth. Her hand tightened around Green-Eyes' cock as heat shot through her, from nipple to vagina. She squeezed Cole's cock within her.

"I think I should make room for our friends," Cole said, and lifted her off him, leaving her with a shocking sense of emptiness, then she felt his cock-head push against her back opening and begin to ease inside, slowly.

Green-Eyes' mouth fell open, but he quickly regained his composure and leaned forward to lick her other nipple. At the feel of both her nipples in hot, moist man-mouths, her eyelids fell closed and she moaned. Cole's cock continued to impale her, pressing into her slowly, widening her tight opening with its passage.

"You are so hot," Blue-Eyes said. He sucked her deep.

Green-Eyes nodded. "How far can we . . . ?" His cheeks flushed red. "I mean . . ."

She smiled and tugged on his cock, pulling him toward her. She lifted her mouth and he leaned in to kiss her. He pressed his lips to hers awkwardly at first, then he slipped his tongue into her mouth. He tasted minty and fresh.

His friend's hand slid down her stomach and over her folds. His fingertip found her clit and stroked it.

"You can go inside if you want." She handed him a condom from the bag, then turned to Blue-Eyes. "You, too." She grinned as she handed him one, too. "I'm sure you can find a way to share."

They quickly tore open the packets and rolled on the ribbed condoms. Blue-Eyes stepped forward and pressed his slender, but longer cock to her opening then slid inside. The feel of two hot hard cocks inside her—Cole in her ass and Blue-Eyes in her vagina—sent her senses reeling. She felt so incredibly full. Blue-Eyes pushed deep into her, then pulled back, then forward again. Green-Eyes looked a little disappointed, but after about four thrusts, his friend slipped out and nodded to Green-Eyes to take his place. Green-Eyes pushed inside her. He wasn't as long as his friend, but he was wider, stretching her with his girth. He stroked several times, then stepped aside for the other man.

They continued this way, first one, then the other, thrusting into her, while Cole remained still inside her, simply filling her, though occasionally he twitched, sending exciting tremors through her. Green-Eyes pushed into her again and stroked. Waves pulsed through her. As Green-Eyes started to pull out, she grabbed his shoulders and pulled him forward. Clinging to him, she pulled him tight against her.

"Fuck me," she murmured in his ear. "Make me come."

His arms went around her and he thrust in and out, deep . . . hard . . . bringing her closer to the edge.

Cole pivoted his hips beneath her, pushing farther into her in short thrusts. The combined sensations exploded through her and she wailed as an orgasm erupted within her.

Green-Eyes tensed, then pulsed into her. He eased out, then Blue-Eyes stepped in and surged into her. His long cock pushed deeper and he thrust, driving her into another orgasm. Cole drove upward and both men groaned at the same time. She gasped and wailed her release.

Their movements slowed and, after a moment, Blue-Eyes pulled out.

"That was incredible," he said.

She smiled at him and Cole's cock slipped free as she stood up. Each man hugged her and gave her an enthusiastic kiss. At the sound of clapping, her gaze shot to the other shore to see two more men watching them, their cocks in their hands and wide smiles on their faces.

"Oh, those are our friends," Green-Eyes said. "They must have come looking for us."

Even though she'd just had two fantastic orgasms, her breasts ached and her vagina clenched in need.

"Invite them over," she said, her voice husky.

Green-Eyes grinned widely.

"Hey, get over here," Blue-Eyes called, waving enthusiastically.

They dove into the water and, as soon as they stepped out, Harmony grabbed the condoms and strolled toward them. She dropped the bag on the ground, then stroked each of their chests. One was tall and broad-shouldered, and built like a football player, his blond hair cropped short, while the other was more slender but tightly muscled with shoulder-length wavy red hair.

She leaned in and kissed one of the men, then the other. She dropped to her knees and slid her hand into the blue bathing suit of the smaller man and wrapped her hand around the cool flesh of his hard cock, then swallowed it into her mouth. The broader man dropped his suit to the ground as he watched her lips surround his friend. She sucked until the cock in her mouth was hard as stone, then turned to the other, which was already halfway there. Like him, his cock was broad and stood very tall. Still pumping the first cock with her hand, she swallowed the tip of this gigantic cock, unsure how much of him she could take. As it swelled, she continued to stroke the other man's cock to keep it ready.

When both cocks were full to bursting, she grabbed two condoms from the bag and handed one to each of them. Once they'd rolled them on, she stood up and stroked her hands over the shoulders of the blond man—the one with the larger physique, and the biggest cock. She tugged his cock toward her and pressed it to her slit. It was massive and stretched her as it slowly eased inside. She clung to his shoulders and gazed at him in wonder as his member filled her as no other cock ever had. Once he'd slid all the way in, he wrapped his arms around her and lifted her. She wrapped her legs around his waist while clinging to his shoulders, allowing his cock to push a little deeper inside.

"Oh, my God, that feels incredible." She stared at him, wide-eyed.

He grinned. "You're not kidding."

She glanced over her shoulder.

"There's room for you, too," she said to his friend.

Eagerly, he stepped up behind her and she felt his cock press against her ass and find her opening. She pressed her muscles outward to release the tightness so he could slip inside. His hands slid around her and cupped her breasts. He teased her nipples as the two of them began to thrust inside her, tentatively at first, then with more gusto as they found their stride.

"Oh, yeah." The feel of being sandwiched between these two men . . . these total strangers . . . turned her on. They wanted her and they were giving her immense, intensely erotic pleasure.

"Fuck me. Hard and fast."

"Oh, God, baby." The one in front drove his cock deeper into her core. "You are smokin' hot."

She squeezed him, tightening her legs around him as his powerful thrusts pressed her harder against the muscular body behind her.

"I'm gonna come," the one behind her said.

The intensely erotic knowledge that she had just made three men come and now another was on the verge sent renewed heat bubbling through her. She squeezed the cock in her vagina and, as the cock behind her pulsed, she exploded in orgasm. The hot cock in front pulsed at the same time and she wailed as he groaned. The three of them continued to move as she moaned in a long, tremendously powerful orgasm.

Harmony stepped from the elevator and walked down the hall to her room, wondering where Aiden was. She pushed the key card into the door, then entered the room and glanced around warily. Aiden wasn't here.

If he had been, would he have been able to tell how she'd spent her afternoon—or at least suspected?

Her body felt gritty. A result of the salt and sand clinging to her after swimming in the ocean—and having sex with five men for most of the afternoon.

She dropped her bag onto the floor and headed straight

for the bathroom. She reached into the shower and turned the water on to warm up, then unwrapped the fuchsia velour towel from her waist and dropped it to the floor. She peeled off her bathing suit and stepped under the warm spray, allowing the sand and salt to wash from her hair and skin. She shampooed her hair thoroughly and scrubbed her body with the tangy, citrus-scented body gel.

She stepped out of the shower smelling clean and fresh. Once she'd finished drying and combing her hair, she wrapped a clean, white towel around herself and stepped into the bedroom.

"Hi."

Aiden sat on the armchair by the window, his hands clasped between his knees.

"Hi," she said. Her fingers clamped over the corner of the towel tucked in front, ensuring it was secure.

"I heard you come in." He waved vaguely at the adjoining door, which stood open.

The door had probably been open when she'd come in—she hadn't thought to check—but then she'd wanted to get cleaned up before she ran into Aiden. She was feeling more than a little guilty about her tryst by the waterfall.

"I'm sorry about earlier . . . about how I acted . . . ," she said.

He stood up and moved toward her.

"It's okay."

"But you were right, I had no right to be jealous if you had sex with your ex—"

He stood in front of her and gazed into her eyes. She felt tears well up as he wrapped his arms around her and pulled her close.

"I didn't have sex with Mia."

She nodded, tears streaming down her face. "Okay." Relief surged through her. "But even if you had . . . or if you do while you're here . . . I have no right to—"

He tipped her chin up and met her watery gaze.

"That's not going to happen." He kissed her, his lips warm and gentle on hers. He grinned at her. "Anyway, those tears of yours are telling me a different story."

"You're being so understanding, but . . ." She wiped the tears away. "These aren't about that . . ."

"What is it, sweetheart?"

"It's . . . something I've done." The tears streamed from her eyes again. "I was so busy accusing you of cheating on me, yet . . . I just cheated on you. Cole and I just—"

He grinned again and kissed her nose. "Harmony, stop worrying. That's why we're here. You and the others in the group—"

"I know, but . . ." She drew away from him and sat on the edge of the bed. "You're okay with the fact I have sex with my friends in the group during the yearly vacations, but . . ."

"But . . . ?" he prompted as he crouched in front of her. As he watched her, his grin faded. "Are you trying to tell me that you are in love with Cole?"

In love with Cole?

"No, of course not."

His grin returned. "Then you didn't cheat on me."

"You don't understand. Cole and I made love under a waterfall. Two guys saw us and then . . ."

"Yes?" His eyes glittered with interest. "Tell me about it."

"Then I . . . sort of . . ." Damn, she didn't want to tell him this. She didn't want to drive him away . . . didn't want to see the look of disgust in his eyes, which would turn to revulsion.

He nodded, encouraging her to continue.

She clutched her hands together. She had to tell him.

"I invited them to join us."

"So you're saying," he began slowly, "that you invited two strange men to have sex with you?"

She nodded, waiting for his anger and disgust.

"Okay, I really need to understand this. So you and Cole were having sex. Were you lying down or sitting?"

"We were sitting. Cole was behind me." She remembered Cole's rigid member sliding in and out of her.

"And the other men just happened to walk by?"

"I saw them standing by the water and I . . ." She twisted her fingers around each other. "Found it really sexy that they were so turned on watching us."

Aiden stroked his fingers down her chest and dipped under the towel, between her breasts.

"I guess they saw your beautiful, naked breasts." He tugged on the towel, easing the tucked corner free. The terry fabric slid downward slowly, revealing the swell of her breasts.

At his seductive tone and the heat simmering in his cinnamon brown eyes, understanding flashed through her. *He's getting turned on by this.* She grasped the edge of the towel, stopping its descent.

"You don't understand. I made love with total strangers."

He grinned. "Oh, I understand." He leaned forward and nuzzled her neck. "And I find it extremely sexy. I love how uninhibited you are."

"How can you be okay with this?" she demanded.

He gently grasped her shoulders. "Harmony, your concern about me making love with Mia is valid. I was involved with her once. I was in love with her, whereas having sex with these men was just a casual act of pleasure." He kissed her temple, then her neck. "An erotic, sexy act that turns me on just thinking about it."

Love. It still hurt to know he'd been in love with the other woman.

He drew her hands from the edge of the towel and drew it open, then his mouth enveloped her nipple. Her fingers twined through his hair as pleasure spiked through her.

"Did Cole stop making love with you to watch?"

"No."

His tongue swirled over her hard, swelling nipple and his hand stroked over her inner thigh. She clung to his head.

"He was making love to me from behind while the men came and stroked my breasts, then sucked on them like you're doing."

"One on each side?" He sucked her nipple while squeezing the other between his finger and thumb.

"Oh, yeah. Then Cole slid out of my vagina and went in behind."

Aiden squeezed tighter. "Really?"

"Then one man slid his cock into me, while the other watched." Her hand slid down Aiden's hard belly and over his incredibly hard cock. "Then they traded . . . back and forth. First one did a couple of strokes, then the other."

"They were both fucking you while Cole fucked you from behind?"

His hand slid between her thighs and stroked along her wet slit.

"That's right. First one, then the other."

"Their long hard cocks sliding into you?"

"That's right. Then one came to orgasm."

"Did you come?"

"Yes." She nodded, concentrating on the delightful sensations thrumming through her as his fingers glided along her slit, then stroked over her clit, then along her wet opening again. She grasped his hard cock and stroked it. Up and down.

"Then the second one came. And I did, too. Again."

"Oh, yeah." He moaned as she squeezed his cock, then stroked under the head.

She pushed herself back on the bed, her legs wide, inviting him. He prowled over her and as he pushed his cock-head to her opening, she said, "Two of their friends heard us and they came over to join us, too."

"Really?" Aiden had been guiding his cock into her slowly, but when she nodded, he thrust forward, impaling her with his erection. She gasped at the exquisite sensation of him stretching her inner passage. He kissed her passionately. "So you had sex with five men today. At one time."

"That's right."

He pulled back and thrust forward again. Pleasure surged through her.

"Once Cole and the other two had come, I went to the two new men and sucked their cocks. One of them was absolutely massive. I could hardly get him in my mouth."

"Really?"

"Then they fucked me front and back at the same time." She could still remember those two cocks gliding in and out of her. Especially that huge cock.

Aiden stroked her hair back from her face and thrust more quickly.

"Oh God, that's so exciting." He kissed her, his gaze locking on hers. "*You* are so exciting."

He thrust deeper and faster. She clung to him, swept away on a searing wave of pleasure. She moaned as her senses exploded in an eruption of bliss.

Aiden tensed and groaned, filling her with white-hot semen.

They lay in each other's arms, gasping for air. So Aiden wasn't disgusted by her, even when she made love with four strangers. She wondered if she'd actually done it to see how far she could push him? Not consciously, of course.

Aiden was a pretty spectacular guy. He seemed to accept her for who she was, not just in the role she'd been playing in her everyday life. And he understood why she was uncomfortable with the thought of him making love with his ex-girlfriend.

The one he'd been in love with. Her heart clenched. The fact that Mia had broken up with him, not the other way around, meant that maybe . . . Was it possible he was still in love with Mia? If Harmony didn't hurry up and accept his proposal, or maybe even if she did, would he consider going back to Mia?

ELEVEN

Cole sat back in his chair and gazed at the lush vista outside his window, framed by palm trees.

Harmony might get married. And, judging from her concerns about how Aiden would feel about the activities of the group, once she did, she probably wouldn't come back. The thought wound through Cole's gut. He couldn't stand the thought of never seeing Harmony again. Never sharing secrets about their lives—things they would never tell anyone else. Never being able to touch her lush body, to sink into her velvet opening.

His cock hardened at the thought of gliding into her. Even though he'd just spent an exciting afternoon of sexual escapades with her, he still couldn't wait until the next time he could make love with her.

But it was about more than sex with her. He cared about her. He loved talking with her, sharing with her. Touching her, kissing her.

He'd never considered taking things further, because it might have scared her off. Put a distance between them. She might even have left the group.

Now it wasn't just a fear—it was a distinct possibility.

At the thought of losing her, a heavy ache bore down on him.

Could it be he was in love with her? Or was he simply afraid he'd never see her again?

Damn it, what was he going to do now?

A knock sounded at the door. Harmony glanced in the mirror and smoothed the bodice of her black dress, then adjusted the halter tie at the back of her neck. She strolled to the door and pulled it open.

"Hi." Nikki looked striking in her form-fitting violet dress, her mass of brown curls tamed into a twist at the back of her head.

Cole stood by her side, devastatingly handsome in his tailored black suit.

"Hi, we're almost ready. Come on in." She stepped aside to let them in. "Aiden will just be a minute." She crossed to the adjoining door and poked her head inside. "Nikki and Cole are here."

"I'll be right there," he called. He stood at the dresser, combing his hair in front of the mirror. The cool thing about adjoining rooms was that it meant two bathrooms, and two showers. Very handy when getting ready to go out.

Nikki and Cole had settled on the couch in the sitting area. Harmony sat down on the armchair across from them.

"So is Aiden psyched for this evening?" Nikki asked.

Harmony tapped her fingers on the arm of the chair.

"I think so, but I'm a little worried about how to ease him into it."

"Going out for a couple of drinks first was a great idea. We'll be in public, no expectations," Cole said.

Nikki grinned. "And I have an idea how to break the ice."

Aiden stepped through the door, smiling. Harmony's heart thrummed. He looked gorgeous in his charcoal suit, which accentuated his broad shoulders and narrow waist.

"Are we all set?" he asked.

Harmony stood up and grabbed her gold-sequined evening bag from the dresser. Nikki followed her, then glanced at Harmony with a sly grin.

"Harmony, what is that?" She stared at Harmony's dress, scrutinizing the fabric across her hips.

"What?" Harmony stared down at her dress, trying to see what Nikki saw.

"I see a panty line."

Harmony glanced in the mirror, but could barely see the line of her skimpy, silk panties.

Nikki stroked her hand over Harmony's derriere. "It totally ruins the line of your dress." She winked at Harmony in the mirror.

Ah, this is Nikki's idea to break the ice.

Harmony widened her eyes in an exaggerated fashion, as if she'd just seen the problem.

"Oh, my. You're right." She stroked her hands along her hips, then turned to see her back in the mirror.

"You know, you should just take them off," Nikki suggested.

Harmony grinned. "You're probably right."

Aiden sat down on the armchair as he and Cole watched the two women.

"Here, let me help you." Nikki slid the hem of Harmony's dress upward, gliding her soft hand along Harmony's thigh. Nikki's fingers caught under the elastic of Harmony's panties and drew them downward. Aiden and Cole stared with intense interest as her black lace panties dropped into sight, Nikki guiding them down Harmony's calves. Harmony lifted one foot out of the panties, then the other. Nikki tossed them casually over her shoulder toward Cole. He smiled as he crumpled them and slid them into his inner jacket pocket.

Nikki turned toward the door, but Harmony caught her arm.

"Wait, Nikki. You have the same problem."

Harmony stepped toward the other woman and stroked over her round, firm behind, then slid the silky fabric of her skirt upward. She reached and found the silk panties underneath and slid them downward and off, then tossed them to Aiden with a wink. The two men were practically drooling.

Nikki smoothed down her skirt and smiled.

"You're right. That's much better," Nikki said. She glanced over her shoulder at the two men. "Coming?"

By the look on their faces, Harmony thought they were probably pretty close. She laughed as she followed Nikki to the door. Harmony was very conscious of the two men watching her and Nikki as they walked down the hallway to the elevator. She felt totally naked from the waist down, even with her gown swirling around her legs.

A few moments later, they stepped into the bar and sat in a cozy, curved booth in a dimly lit corner.

Nikki grabbed Aiden's hand.

"Why don't you sit beside me?" Nikki sent him an inviting smile. "Then Harmony, then Cole."

Cole sat beside Harmony, leaving her sandwiched between the two men. Harmony was aware of Cole's hard, muscular thigh pressed the length of her left leg and Aiden's pressed against her right leg.

A waitress came by and took their drink orders. The soft sounds of a bass played in the background, joined by the gentle notes of a piano. The drinks arrived and Harmony took a long sip of the house specialty drink, savoring the tangy mango flavor.

Nikki rested her elbow on the table and leaned toward Aiden as she twirled her straw in her orange-and-red tropical drink.

"Aiden, you must find this whole thing a little strange. The way we in the group all . . . share so much."

He smiled. "Not at all."

Harmony watched Nikki's hand disappear under the table and she couldn't be sure, but from the angle of Nikki's shoulder and the way she leaned slightly forward, Harmony was pretty sure Nikki had her hand on Aiden's thigh.

"So you're not finding it too overwhelming?" Cole asked.

"Actually, I find the whole business absolutely fascinating," Aiden answered. "Especially a little adventure she had this afternoon."

The two men's gazes locked and tension rose in Harmony, but then Cole laughed.

"Yes, Harmony is an adventurous one."

Aiden sensed Harmony's tension, even though his hormones were being pelted by the feel of Nikki's warm hand on his thigh, and the knowledge that Harmony—and Nikki—were both panty-less under their sexy dresses.

He focused on Harmony. She was worried about his reaction to her friends and the whole sexual situation, especially tonight on this double date they'd set up to ease him into the group activities. He rested his hand on her thigh and gave her a reassuring squeeze, then remembered again that she had no panties on. His hand stroked upward of its own accord, gliding toward her inner thigh . . . then brushed against another male hand. Cole's.

Aiden drew his hand away, but he sent a reassuring smile Harmony's way. It was odd feeling another man touching his girlfriend, but he'd signed on for this adventure and he would follow through.

"What happened this afternoon?" Nikki asked with an inquisitive smile.

Aiden felt Nikki's fingers tighten around his thigh, then slide upward a little. His groin tightened in anticipation.

"Later," Harmony replied.

"Well, at least tell me the jist of it."

Aiden chuckled.

"Suffice it to say that Harmony entertained a few male admirers," Cole said.

"Ohhhh. . . ." Nikki's eyes lit up and her hand crept higher up Aiden's thigh. "How many?"

"Four," Harmony said quickly, clearly wishing Nikki's questioning would stop.

"You forgot one," Aiden corrected, grinning.

Harmony glanced at Cole and she actually blushed. Aiden chuckled. She'd have wild sex in public with five men but blush when teased about it by a woman she'd been sharing three men—and another woman—with for over a decade.

How did it work with the two women, he wondered, not for the first time.

Harmony's fingers clutched her glass. "Let's change the topic."

"What do you suggest?" Cole asked.

"I know." Nikki grinned impishly. "Oops, my napkin fell on the floor." She leaned toward Aiden, her soft, warm body pressed against his side as she reached under the table in front of him. But she bypassed his tightening cock and he felt her hand glide up Harmony's leg.

When she sat upright again, she leaned toward Aiden and the others.

"You know," she murmured, "I do believe Harmony's dress rode up somehow and now her pussy is completely exposed. Aiden, I think you should slide your hand up her thigh. And you, too, Cole. I bet she'd like to feel both your fingers sliding into her." She winked. "You know . . . to keep her warm."

The thought sent Aiden's cock to full attention. Nikki's hand slid from his leg and she shifted a little in her seat.

"In fact, it seems the same thing has happened to my dress and . . ."

She grasped Aiden's hand and guided it to her thigh. As she slid it up her silky flesh, she murmured in his ear. "Don't forget Harmony."

His left hand shifted to Harmony's thigh and slid upward. The feel of two women under his hands sent his pulse racing. When he reached Harmony's pussy, he bumped into Cole's hand, already gliding between her folds. His other hand reached Nikki's curls and he slid into her hot, wet slit. His other index finger joined Cole's inside Harmony.

Harmony almost gasped at the feel of both men inside her. Cole's finger slid out and stroked over her clit. Her hand fell to his thigh and she squeezed. From the look of delight on Nikki's face, Aiden was stroking her, too.

Harmony had both men pleasuring her and Aiden was pleasuring both women.

Oh, God, it didn't get any better than this.

As Cole teased her clit with his fingertip, Aiden slid in two more fingers and twirled them to and fro. It was so good. So—

Pleasure spiked through her and she squeezed Cole's thigh even tighter. Nikki sucked in air and her eyes rolled back. Harmony glanced around, but no one seemed to notice them in their corner booth. Aiden slid out as Cole slid inside her again. Aiden swirled over her clit and Cole dove in deep, then thrust gently. The pleasure overwhelmed her and she moaned. Her eyelids, which had been half-mast, popped open and scanned the crowd, but no one had heard.

An orgasm blasted through her and she clamped down on the moan wanting to burst from her. She rode the wave of pleasure, noticing Nikki slumped back in the seat, clearly nearing orgasm herself. Finally, Harmony let her eyelids fall shut as she, too, slumped back on the seat and gave herself over to the bliss. Quietly.

"Would you like another?" a female voice said.

Harmony's eyelids snapped open and she stared at the waitress.

"What?"

The woman gestured toward her glass. "Another drink?"

Harmony shook her head, then pushed herself up in the seat.

"I think we're done here," Nikki said as she pushed aside her empty glass.

Harmony nodded and gulped down the last bit of her drink.

Ten minutes later, she and the others followed Cole into his room, which was totally different and much larger than Harmony's. They stepped into a large, comfortable sitting area with a bar along one side, complete with leather uphol-stered stools, and a huge window with a view of the ocean. There were two closed doors, probably leading to a separate bedroom and bathroom.

Harmony sat in one of the easy chairs, while Aiden sat on the couch beside Nikki. Cole chose the chair across from Harmony.

"Aiden, I know this must be strange for you—even if you like the idea," Nikki said. "Why don't you let us make it a little easier for you?"

He raised an eyebrow and Harmony knew he was in-trigued.

"How?"

"Well, let's imagine that Harmony is my slave. She must do everything I tell her to do."

Harmony smiled. Trust Nikki to figure out a way to make this work.

"Harmony," she said in an authoritative voice. "Sit on the stool." She gestured to the leather-upholstered stools by the bar off the comfy sitting area.

Obediently, Harmony stood up and walked toward the stool, then sat atop it. It was a high stool, so she hooked her high heels behind the lower cross bar.

Nikki followed and stepped behind her. Harmony felt her

fingers at the back of her neck and, a second later, her halter top dropped forward. Cool air washed across her bare breasts. Nikki's hand slid under Harmony's breasts and she lifted them a little.

"Don't these look tempting?" she asked. Her thumb stroked over one nipple and it sprang to attention.

Both men strode forward and cupped her breasts in their strong, masculine hands.

"Oh, I have an idea," Nikki said and she scooted into the bedroom and returned a moment later with a sleep mask, which she slid over Harmony's eyes.

The men's hands released her, Nikki giggled, and Harmony heard shuffling. Then a mouth covered her nipple and she gasped. She had no idea whose mouth it was. A moment later, another mouth covered her other nipple and sucked hard.

Two pairs of hands, one masculine and one feminine, eased her thighs apart. Fingers—from several hands—stroked up her inner thighs. A third mouth covered her navel, then a tongue lightly teased it. Then it moved downward as the other mouths continued to suck and lick her tight nipples. The tongue lapped over her clit and she gasped.

The nibbles on her left breast seemed gentler and the lips soft, so she thought that was Nikki, but she wasn't sure. The mouth down below moved on her, gliding along her slit, teasing her clit, then the tongue dove into her folds.

"Oh, yes."

She felt a hand on her lower back.

"Move forward, Harmony," Nikki said. The mouth on her left breast had disappeared for a moment—so it was Nikki.

Harmony shifted to the edge of the seat . . . and felt something firm and hot press against her folds. Her hand sought the cock. It pressed into her, the head pushing against her, then easing forward a tiny bit.

"Wait. Not yet," Nikki interrupted.

Harmony gritted her teeth. She was so ready for the hot invasion.

The wonderful cock slipped away, then so did both hot mouths, leaving her nipples tingling in the relatively cool air.

Nikki grasped Harmony's shoulders and guided her a couple of steps from the stool, then turned her around. She eased her forward again, then took Harmony's hand. A second later, she felt her fingers wrapped around a hot, hard cock. She squeezed it as Nikki placed her other hand around another erection.

Harmony stroked both of them, gliding their lengths. She knew exactly which was which. Cole's wide, veined cock was in her left hand, and Aiden's slightly longer, smoother cock was in her right.

"Harmony, I want you to suck Cole, then Aiden," Nikki instructed.

Purposely, Harmony leaned toward the wrong cock first, easing her face toward her hand, then wrapping her lips around Aiden's thick cock-head. She stroked her tongue around the underside, then sucked. She released him and eased toward the other, finding it and sucking it deep into her mouth.

"Scooch together," Nikki said.

She pulled off Harmony's blindfold and Harmony saw the two gorgeous cocks staring straight at her. Cole's thick and purple nested in dark curls. Aiden's longer with a more bulbous head, protruding from a less dense patch of brown hair. She bobbed up and down, first on one, then on the other.

"Oh, yes, you've got them good and hard now," Nikki complimented. "Step back, let me see."

Nikki grasped each one and stroked. "Yes, quite nice."

She stood in front of Harmony. "Unzip my dress."

Harmony slid the zipper down and Nikki dropped the dress on the floor. Since she wore no panties or bra, she now stood naked in front of the two men. Harmony's dress still hung on her like a skirt, with the top draped down like an apron.

Nikki stepped forward and thrust her breasts toward Aiden. He took the hint and one hard little nub disappeared into his mouth. Cole stroked his hand over her round derriere.

"Mmm. You two are very good. You both deserve a reward."

She stepped back and gestured for the men to stand up. They obeyed as quickly as Harmony had.

"I think you should remove my slave's dress."

Aiden drew the short zipper downward and Cole eased the dress past her hips. It fell to the floor.

"Slave, sit." She pointed at the top of a stool.

Harmony climbed into position, anticipation careening through her.

Nikki put the sleep mask back in place, returning Harmony to darkness. Again, her legs were eased open and hard thighs brushed against them. Hardness pressed against her moist slit and the cock eased forward. Relentlessly. Gliding into her hot, wet flesh.

He pushed in to the hilt, and stood still for a second, then slid back. And out. She whimpered. His heat slipped away, then returned. No, she was pretty sure this was the other man. A new, hot cock pressed into her, then slid inside.

"Oh, yes." She stroked her hand down his chest. Smooth, satin flesh drawn taut over soild muscle.

Cole.

Then he slid out and away.

Another cock pressed against her. Cole again? Or Aiden? She resisted touching his body. She didn't want to know.

The cock slid into her. Then out.

It was sexy not knowing.

A pause. Then a cock slid in again.

One then the other. In and out.

Her breathing accelerated.

"You two are doing such a good job." Nikki sounded a little breathless. "I think I need some attention now."

Another cock slid into Harmony as rustling sounds and a feel of heat beside her told her that Nikki was on the stool next to her.

The cock impaling her slid outward, but didn't exit. It thrust forward again. Strong masculine arms came around her and she slid her hands around his neck as the cock pulled back and thrust forward again.

"Oh, baby, that is some powerful-looking cock you've got there." Nikki giggled. "Yeah, bring it right over here."

The man inside Harmony kissed her temple, then his cock drove in deeper. He thrust again and again. Pleasure swept through her. Nikki's gasps of pleasure beside her heightened the sensations.

"Oh, yeah, just like that." Nikki moaned. "Honey . . . uh huh . . . I'm going to . . . oh, yeah . . . I'm going to come." She moaned.

The hot, hard cock drove into Harmony and she was so close.

"Slave, come," Nikki commanded, then she wailed in climax.

Harmony felt hot pleasure erupt inside her and she clung to the strong shoulders in front of her.

"That's right, sweetheart. Come for me," Cole murmured in her ear.

Aiden's release was hot and fast as soon as Nikki moaned her pleasure and squeezed around him. He glanced at Harmony and a flash of jealousy dashed through him at the look of utter bliss on her face. She and Cole looked very right together.

And that felt entirely wrong to Aiden.

What the hell was wrong with him? He'd just screwed

the delightful Nikki right beside Harmony. Harmony didn't even know who was screwing her right this instant. Did she? She hadn't been able to tell whose cock she was sucking when Nikki had instructed her to suck first Cole's then Aiden's.

So there was nothing to be jealous about. For all she knew, he was the one fucking her right now.

And that didn't even matter. The whole idea was she enjoyed sex with all three men in the group. But he was the one she was with in real life.

TWELVE

Mia's stomach tied into knots as she entered the dining room. She hated eating alone. She hadn't wanted to come down at all, thinking she'd just have room service, but by about nine she'd finally decided she'd go nuts cooped up all alone. Being around other people, even if they were at other tables was better than sitting in her room alone.

What had she been thinking coming all the way to the Caribbean after Aiden? Clearly, he loved this new woman of his. Clearly, he didn't want Mia back—which sent her ego crashing down around her ankles.

She had really believed he'd be happy to see her—that he'd want her back. After all, he'd loved her so much. He'd shown that in so many ways.

She remembered when she'd been house-sitting at her brother's isolated home in the country and she'd woken up at 4 A.M. to see a red light on the alarm system. She'd listened intently for any sounds of an intruder. The house was big and strange and every noise sounded threatening. She'd gotten herself all worked up and finally snatched up the phone and called Aiden. Even though he'd had to start work at 9 A.M. the next morning, he'd talked to her until she'd calmed down, then made the forty-five-minute drive to spend the rest of the night with her. She'd felt so cherished and protected sleeping in his arms.

The next evening, Aiden had figured out the light simply indicated an interruption in the security service when the Internet-based phone service it relied on had gone down briefly. He'd spent every night with her for the rest of the week so she wouldn't be all alone.

She'd been a fool to break up with him. It had been so wonderful basking in the warmth of his love—his adoration.

The problem was, she'd never felt she quite deserved him—or the intense love he held for her.

When Craig had come into her life, the attraction of a new love had turned her head. The fact that someone else wanted her boosted her ego. But she'd never really loved Craig—and obviously he hadn't loved her or he wouldn't have dumped her for another woman.

Now Mia realized what she'd had with Aiden. She'd decided to push aside her insecurities about deserving his love, and she kept telling herself her doubts about her feelings for him were just a different form of insecurity. After all, how could any woman know when she'd met Mr. Right? All new lovers sent tingles through you and sent your heartbeat into double-time. Infatuation wasn't hard to recognize. It was love that was difficult.

But she loved Aiden. The fact that she'd longed for him as soon as she found herself alone was a sure sign.

So she'd had to take a shot. For both their sakes.

Maybe he loved this other woman.

Or . . . maybe he just needed time to think about it. Mia had decided she would stay the week—that would give him time to change his mind. . . .

Not that she wanted to break up a relationship—but it would be better for all of them in the long run if it ended now, rather than Aiden wishing he'd made a different choice *after* the wedding.

But for now she was alone.

And she *hated* being alone.

The hostess approached her.

"Are you waiting for someone?" she asked.

Mia shook her head and followed the hostess past tables of happy diners at candlelit tables. Sipping wine. Sampling delectable gourmet food. Sharing the companionship of friends or lovers.

Mia sighed.

"Mia?"

At the sound of a woman's voice calling her name, she glanced around to see three familiar smiling faces at a table off to her right. These were the people Aiden had been sitting with last evening.

The woman gestured her toward the table and one of the two men, the blond one with the diamond earring—Trey, that was his name—said, "Mia, why don't you join us?"

The hostess tipped her head in question and Mia smiled.

"That would be wonderful. Thank you."

Trey smiled as he pulled out a chair for her and she sat down. She couldn't help but notice his broad shoulders and strong arms. His chocolate brown eyes shimmering with flecks of gold and warm smile made her feel welcome . . . and also unsettled her a little—in a good way. He was a very attractive man.

The hostess placed the menu in front of her.

"This is very nice of you. I hate eating alone." She smiled at the other two people. The man with light brown hair pulled back in a short ponytail and a coarse shadow across his jaw, and the woman with long blond hair arranged in an elegant coil at the back of her head. Darn, Mia couldn't remember their names.

"Oh, don't think anything of it, honey," the blond woman said. "I'm the same way."

Trey grinned at the woman. "Alone is definitely not Angela's style."

Angela leaned toward him and stroked her hand along his cheek.

"That's so true." She turned and winked at Mia. "And, luckily, with Jake and Trey, I don't have to be."

Trey and Jake. What kind of relationship did these three share exactly?

"Where is your other friend?" she asked. "The woman who wore the royal blue halter dress?" she added, in case they thought she meant Aiden or his girlfriend.

"Oh, Nikki's got plans with friends tonight." Angela smiled impishly. "And she left me all alone to entertain these two." She grinned and patted Mia's hand. "But now you can help me with that."

"Which we appreciate," Trey said, sending Mia a warm smile.

She felt a soft blush creep across her cheeks.

"Not that we weren't totally enthralled by Angela's company." He stroked Angela's bare forearm and the fine hairs prickled to attention.

Mia was a little confused. Trey seemed to be flirting with her yet there was a definite bond between him and Angela. An affection that seemed more than just friendship. Mia couldn't tell how much more.

And at the same time, Angela was definitely flirting with Jake.

The waitress came to take their order.

"Go ahead and order," Mia said as she quickly perused the menu. "I'll be ready in just a second."

When the waitress got to her, she ordered a shrimp cocktail and filet of sole with a salad. Trey ordered a bottle of white wine for the table.

Mia spent the whole of dinner trying to figure out the relationship dynamics between her three companions. Angela's carefree attitude and the way she touched each of the men—the way she rested her hand on one's arm, the way she leaned in to murmur into the other's ear—and myriad other subtle actions . . . all gave Mia the impression that she'd been intimate with both of them, yet neither of the men seemed jealous of the other. They had to be aware of the same not-so-subtle indications.

"So you came on vacation alone?" Angela asked as Trey filled Mia's glass with more wine, then topped up Angela's and Jake's. "That's adventurous of you."

Mia twined her fingers together. "Not really. My friend got sick at the last minute and couldn't come."

It wasn't true, of course. But Mia wouldn't tell anyone else that. They'd think her desperate—and mean for trying to break up a couple, even though she was just following her heart.

"Well, her misfortune is our good luck." Trey smiled at her as she sipped her wine.

As the warmth of the liquid heated her insides, she gazed into Trey's warm brown eyes—so much like Aiden's.

Heavens, Trey was a sexy man. She wanted to reach out and stroke back his fashionably tousled, dark blond hair, to run her hand over his broad shoulders, to feel the hardness of his muscles under her fingers.

"So all of you knew each other in college?" she asked. "And now you vacation together once a year?"

"That's right." Angela smiled. "And I look forward to it all year."

"You must be a pretty close group."

Jake chuckled, a deep masculine sound. "Yeah, pretty close." He stroked his hand along Angela's shoulders.

Actually, Mia was getting an idea of just how close. They were obviously here for sexual escapades . . . and since they were short one player, she got the impression they were trying to draw her in. For tonight anyway. Once their friend, Nikki, was back in the fold, they'd probably dump Mia on the spot.

"So your friend Nikki and the three of you . . . are you two couples?"

"No," Trey answered, picking up her hand and stroking the insides of her fingers, sending tingles through her. "We're all single."

"So this special relationship you all have together . . . I take it you're all involved . . . sexually."

Even as she was saying it, she felt it was an odd observation and she was sure they'd deny it . . . even if it was true.

The three of them stared at each other and, at the uncomfortable silence, Mia shook her head.

"I'm sorry. I'm sure I misread the whole situation."

"No, not at all." Trey held her hand. He glanced at the other two and Angela nodded her head. "We've been meeting for over ten years now and we enjoy open, adventurous sex with one another. For one glorious week every year, we leave our regular, straightlaced lives behind and become sexual adventurers. With a group of people we love and trust."

A safe and loving environment to explore their sexuality. Now past her initial shock, Mia felt a deep longing. To be a part of a group like this...where she would be totally accepted...year after year. No fear of rejection or the inevitable end of the relationship.

"How did you ever start a group like that?"

"In college," Jake said. "Trey and I were actually a couple."

"You were gay?" Mia glanced from one sexy, masculine face to the other. They certainly seemed to like women now.

"We weren't really sure," Trey answered. "We were young and trying to figure things out. We were attracted to each other, so we were together. It was as simple as that."

Mia nodded, but she couldn't really believe anything sexual could be as simple as that.

"In our third year, when we moved from a one-bedroom apartment to a town house, we needed two more roommates."

"That's when they met me and Nikki." Angela grinned. "I knew Cole from our computer science class and he knew Nikki and I were looking for a place, so he suggested we move in with Jake and Trey. Of course, he told us they were gay."

"Well, he thought we were," Jake said. "We didn't hide the fact we were together."

"Anyway, Nikki and I moved in and, about a month later, Trey walked in on me in the bathroom. I was stark naked, ready to take a shower, and he had on a bathrobe. The next thing I knew, his erection was staring me straight in the face. I hadn't had sex in a while and he was clearly interested, so I jumped him."

"I heard the noise and went in to see what was happening," Jake said, "and soon I was fucking Angela from behind."

"When I told Nikki about the great threesome, she drooled." Angela grinned. "Soon the four of us were enjoying very friendly—and extremely hot—sex together."

A threesome! Mia felt like drooling herself.

"It didn't take long to get Cole and Harmony into the picture," Trey said. "Those two had a major attraction to each other, but could never manage to get it together. When it became a matter of friendship mixed with hot, hungry sex, they were finally able to get over it and get together."

"We had such a great time, we knew we couldn't let it end when we graduated," Angela said, "so we arranged to keep meeting once a year."

"Wow." Mia wrapped her fingers around her glass. "That's incredible." She took a sip of her wine. "So how does it work exactly? Do you switch rooms each night?" She imagined them all gathered in a room deciding who would go off with whom tonight. Of course, from what they'd said, they didn't restrict themselves to couples. "But you said you sometimes ... uh ... have more than two of you ... together." Her cheeks heated at the clumsiness of her words, but she was enthralled by the possibilities.

Trey chuckled. "Yes, definitely."

"But it's more than just going off to bed at night," Angela said. "It's pushing the envelope. Allowing sex to be a part of everything we do."

Mia's eyes widened. "What do you mean?"

"Well, like right now. Jake's hand is gliding up my thigh . . . under my skirt." Angela shifted in her seat and Mia imagined Angela was parting her legs. Her eyelids dropped closed for a moment and, as they opened, a half smile formed on her lips. When she opened her eyes again, they looked dreamy and slightly out of focus.

Mia leaned toward Trey. "Is he really . . . ?"

Trey nodded. "Oh, yeah."

"Would you like something to drink?"

The sound of the waitress's voice behind her startled Mia. Her gaze jerked to Angela again, but Angela's smile never faded.

"I'm fine," Angela responded, her voice deep and throaty.

Jake and Trey both ordered something, but Mia was too fascinated by Angela's calm countenance, even though Jake's fingers were probably deeply buried in the moistness between her legs. Stroking. Mia felt her own insides start to melt.

"And you, Miss?" the waitress asked Mia.

"Uh, a wine spritzer, please."

Once the waitress left, Angela purred. Mia could tell her breathing was increasing in speed, her chest rising and falling quickly and, after a few moments, she seemed to tense, suck in air, and her eyes rolled back.

"Ohhh," she murmured in a subdued fashion, then she sank back in the chair.

Mia glanced around, but no one seemed to have noticed Angela's quiet orgasm.

"I don't know about the rest of you," Angela said after a few moments, "but I'm ready to change scenery."

Mia followed behind Angela and Jake, Trey trailing behind her, his hand lightly touching her back, as Angela led them up an escalator to the conference level. Angela strolled to the railing overlooking the lobby and leaned against it.

Mia glanced down at the large, elegant lobby adorned with tropical plants with colorful foliage and blossoms, people moving in various directions, some in classy evening attire, others casually donning shorts or track pants. Two couples passing a large red-blossomed plant wore bathing suits with towels wrapped around their waists. Given that it was almost eleven, they must be returning from the pool since it closed in a few minutes.

"Come on." Angela was on the move again.

As Mia and the others followed her toward the elevators, Angela grabbed Jake's hand and, giggling, tugged him sideways. Mia halted as the two of them disappeared behind a large plant. She glanced at Trey hesitantly. He just shrugged and stood beside her.

Beyond the foliage, Mia could see Jake kissing Angela as she leaned against the wall. The plant didn't really hide them as much as put them out of obvious view, but anyone passing by . . .

Oh, goodness.

Mia's heartbeat raced as she saw Angela pull her plunging

neckline aside to bare one of her breasts. Jake stroked it, lifting its weight in his hand, then he leaned in and licked the tip. Mia's breasts tingled at the sight of his mouth covering Angela's nipple.

Angela's chest thrust forward as she unfastened the back of her gown. The fabric fell forward, then hung at her waist. Jake stroked her second bared breast as he continued to lick and suck her nipple.

The sound of people behind her jarred Mia's gaze from the scene. She glanced at the party of five people approaching, then to Trey. He just smiled. She felt her cheeks heat as she realized the people would see Angela and Jake. And they would wonder why Mia was standing here . . . they'd know she was with the indiscreet couple . . . or maybe they'd think she was watching them . . . getting vicarious thrills at being a voyeur.

Seeing her consternation, Trey moved close to her.

"If you're worried about them seeing, let's create a distraction," he suggested. His arms went around her and he drew her to his body. His face approached hers and she knew he intended to kiss her. Her heart thumped loudly in her chest as she realized she wanted him to.

What began as a soft brush of lips quickly grew heated. He groaned in her mouth and pulled her tighter to his body. The feel of hard chest muscles pressed against her soft breasts, of his strong arms wrapped around her, made her feel soft and feminine. His mouth moved on hers and she barely noticed the twittering of laughter and some murmured voices as the people passed by, barely three feet from them, then turned down the elevator corridor.

At the ding of the elevator, followed by the sound of their voices muffled behind closing doors, Trey drew back and smiled down at her. She gazed into his warm brown eyes.

"I don't think they noticed Angela and Jake."

She nodded, wishing more people would come by so he could continue their kiss. A moan from behind the plant grabbed Mia's attention and she glanced around to see Jake still sucking on Angela's breast, but his hand had slid under her skirt and . . .

Angela moaned softly as her face contorted in blissful pleasure. Mia glanced at Trey, her cheeks burning. To her surprise, he was watching her, not the erotic scene playing out only a few yards away.

"Come on, let's go call for the elevator. They'll catch up."

She followed him around the corner and he pushed the call button. A moment later, Jake and Angela came around the corner, Angela smoothing down her skirt. A ding sounded as an arrow lit up over the elevator behind them. The doors opened, revealing that it was one of the glass elevators. They all stepped inside.

"Where to?" Jake asked.

"How about my room?" Angela suggested. "I have a great balcony overlooking the ocean." She pushed the button for the seventeenth floor.

As the elevator began to rise, Angela turned to the glass to stare outside. Jake stood behind her and cupped both her breasts in his big, masculine hands. Anyone glancing in their direction would be able to see what was happening, not that it was likely anyone could see in this high from the ground.

Obviously, Angela wasn't worried about it. Mia sucked in a breath. *So why am I?*

"The view is glorious," Mia said, shifting her attention to the vista below. The light from the nearly full moon illuminated the gardens and stone patio that led to the beach. Moonlight glittered on the ocean as it washed along the white sandy beach.

The elevator stopped and a few moments later, she and the two men followed Angela into her room. When Mia stepped inside, she was amazed at how large the room was. Her own room was a typical hotel room, although nicely appointed, with a bed, desk, TV armoire, a chair and side table, and a bathroom. This room had a large sitting area with a couch, two chairs, and a large, flat TV mounted on the wall. The bed was big and cozy-looking and an inviting hot tub, big enough for at least two people, sat in the corner. Large patio doors framed a beautiful view of the glowing full moon amidst the navy sky studded with stars.

Angela slid open the door and stepped outside. As Mia followed her, curious to see the view of the ocean, she was assailed by the sound of loud music and raucous laughter. Angela leaned against the wooden railing and stared down. Mia followed suit, watching the waves roll along the glittering moonlit beach.

"Hey, ladies, want some company?" called a young man's voice over the loud music, accompanied by hoots and laughter.

Mia glanced toward the balcony to the right and saw several young men, college-aged, grinning at them.

Angela, ignoring the fellows, nudged Mia and whispered, "Want to have some fun?"

"What kind of fun?" she asked, not sure she was ready for the answer.

"Teasing them." Still acting as if she hadn't heard a sound from the men, Angela unfastened her dress and dropped it to the ground, leaving her standing in only a black lace thong.

Wolf whistles sounded from the nearby balcony. Mia backed away and disappeared into the room. Angela sat down on one of the lounge chairs, still facing the balcony's edge and began stroking her breasts. The sounds from the balcony diminished and Mia, although she couldn't see the young guys, could just imagine that they were watching with their tongues hanging out.

Trey slid his arm around Mia as the two of them watched Angela.

"Want a drink?" Jake asked as he set down a bucket full of ice. He must have gone out to get it while Mia was outside with Angela.

Jake picked up the bottle of rum—one of several bottles of liquor and wine that Angela had on the dresser, along with several cans of soft drinks.

"I'll have a rum and Coke," Mia said.

Trey went over and poured himself a drink. Jake handed Mia a glass. The ice cubes tinkled as she took a sip, her gaze glued to the sexy view of Angela stroking one breast as her other hand glided down her belly toward the black lace V of her thong.

"Angela does like to be the center of attention," Trey said as he returned to Mia's side. The glint in his eyes as he watched her showed more than a hint of affection for the other woman.

"That's our Angie all right," Jake added. "She'll drive those young guys crazy before she finally gives them what they want."

"You mean, she's actually going to . . . ?"

Trey nodded. "Sure. Why not?"

"But she doesn't even know them."

Jake grinned. "That's part of the fun."

The young men had fallen totally silent as Angela's fingers dipped under her panties. The thin fabric rippled as her fingers wriggled underneath.

Finally, she turned to face the other balcony for the first time.

"I could really use a man to help me out."

"How about me?" one voice strained.

"No, me," said another.

Angela grinned. "How many are you over there?"

"Six," one called out.

"Well, that should be just enough."

"You're kidding?" one incredulous voice asked.

"Oh, baby, we'll be right over," said another.

"Not here," Angela said, shooting a quick glance through the window to Mia and winking. "Down at the hot tub."

"But it's closed," one of them said.

Angela stood up, smiling, her finger outlining the pebbled aureole of her right breast. "Don't tell me you're going to let a little fence stop you."

She turned toward the door and slid it open. "Fifteen minutes. If you're not there, I'll start without you."

THIRTEEN

Mia's eyes widened as Angela entered the room, then slid the door closed behind her. This woman was so . . . so . . . adventurous. The thought of six young studs . . . naked . . . eager . . . ready to pleasure her. She found it hard to catch her breath.

Angela slipped on a terry robe and grabbed a large, straw bag.

"You boys will entertain Mia until I get back, won't you?"

"Of course," Jake said. "But I bet you'll be entertaining all of us, right?"

She winked as she sashayed to the door. "You know it." She closed the door behind her.

"What does he mean by that?" Mia asked Trey.

Trey stepped to the TV and turned it on, then flipped to a channel that didn't show up on the TV in Mia's room. She had tried them all last night once she'd found herself alone and lonely in her room, after talking to Aiden. On hers, that particular channel showed static, but on this large, high-definition TV, it showed a black screen.

"It doesn't look very interesting," she pointed out.

"Give her a minute to get there," Jake said.

"Jake brought a couple of wireless webcams that can transmit an encrypted signal to the laptop. Angela has them in her bag and she'll set them up when she gets down there so they can send a video stream to the laptop," Trey explained.

Mia noticed a laptop on the desk with a wire connecting it to the TV. Jake tapped at the keyboard.

The TV screen flickered, then Mia could make out a vague dark picture of plants. A second later, the picture brightened.

"She's turning on the lights around the hot tub."

Now Mia could see a clear picture of Angela standing in front of the hot tub waving at them. Or rather, at the camera. Angela shed her robe and turned around, then stepped to the left of the hot tub. The plants Mia had noticed earlier were on the other side of the hot tub from the camera. Angela pulled a small camera from her bag and placed it in the bushes. Jake tapped on the laptop keyboard, and the TV screen flickered again. The picture divided into two, one half showing the original view and the other showing a new view from the second camera Angela had turned on.

"We can watch both views at the same time," Trey said, "or zoom in on one or the other." To illustrate, he picked up the remote control on the dresser below the TV and pressed some buttons. The first view disappeared and the second filled the screen.

"Isn't she worried someone will see them and report them to the management?" Mia asked.

"The hot tub is closed and it's not visible from the hotel," Jake explained.

A moment later, they could hear the sound of voices and laughter and the young men appeared on the screen. First two, then a third and fourth, then all six. Some wore bathing trunks, with the resort-supplied white towels slung over their shoulders or draped loosely around their hips, and some wore shorts and T-shirts.

"There you are." Angela tucked her fingers under the elastic of her thong and slid it down, then kicked it aside. She placed her hands on her hips, facing the current camera, and smiled.

"Oh, baby, you are so hot." A tall, blond fellow eyed her breasts hungrily.

"Honey," she responded. "Don't keep me waiting."

Another man slipped behind her and cupped her breasts, then groaned in pleasure.

The blond pushed the interloper's hands aside and stroked her breasts, then crouched down and licked her nipples, then began to fondle and kiss them. The other one drew her back against his chest and kissed her neck. Tingles danced along Mia's spine and her nipples thrummed with need. She could almost feel the cock of the one behind Angela swell, pressing against her behind. He stroked over her naked buttocks. His hand fiddled between their bodies, then his hot, naked shaft pressed between her thighs. His pelvis rocked forward and his cock stroked her wet slit.

The other four men stared dumbfounded at the sexy sight in front of them.

"I want one of you to eat me," she announced.

She eased away from the two hot guys and walked to the hot tub. She pulled a strip of condoms from her bag then sat down on the edge of the hot tub, dangling her legs in the water.

One fellow with dark shoulder-length hair leaped into the tub, clothing and all, and knelt down in front of her. All Mia could see was the back of his head diving between Angela's legs.

"Turn on the other view," Jake said and Trey flicked a button.

Now Mia could see a side view of the young man licking Angela's slit. The other young men gathered around behind her, watching as their companion pleasured Angela. Many male hands stroked over her body, tweaking her breasts, gliding over her buttocks, stroking her back and stomach.

Trey led Mia to the couch where they could see the sexy images. She sank down beside him on the comfy cushions as her gaze remained locked on Angela and her young companions. Jake sat down on the other side of Mia.

She felt her breasts swell as she watched the one man lick

Angela's clit while the others stroked her. One leaned forward and sucked on one of Angela's generous breasts.

The sight of the young man's head delving into her slit so enthusiastically made Mia's vagina clench with need. She grabbed her drink, which Trey had placed on the coffee table in front of them, and took a generous gulp. Tinkling ice and the heat suffusing her throat all added to the sensory assault already overwhelming her.

Another man leaned over Angela and kissed her on the mouth while the two others dropped their pants and sat on the side of the hot tub. Their cocks stood long and hard and they wrapped their hands around them and stroked as they watched their companions pleasure Angela. She arched and wailed as the long-haired fellow brought her to orgasm.

He smiled up at her and she held out her hand. He helped her to her feet.

"Sit," she said. "All of you. Along the side."

They sat in a row along the side, six erections pointing straight up. Angela leaned over the first one and swallowed it into her mouth.

Mia watched in fascination as Angela progressed along the lineup, bringing each one to climax. As she sucked the fourth one into her mouth, Mia could imagine the feel of the long, hard cock slipping into her own mouth, gliding between her tongue and the roof of her mouth. One of the other men slid behind Angela and cupped her breasts.

Mia's hand slipped under her bodice and flicked over her

aching nipple. Without really thinking about it, she clutched Trey's hand and brought it to her other breast. His strong fingers found her nipple and tweaked it through the fabric. Heat flooded through her.

The man under Angela groaned and jerked and Angela gulped, then moved on to number five. Another man stood behind Angela and stroked her round behind. His finger stroked between her cheeks then slipped inside her vagina.

Mia rested her hand on Trey's and pressed it tighter against her breast. He tried to slide under her bodice but couldn't, so he reached for her zipper and slid it down. Mia quickly shed the dress and sat down between the two men again. Trey flicked open her bra and she tossed it to the floor. She was extremely conscious of the fact she now sat here, her breasts totally naked in front of *two* men. Jake unzipped his jeans and pulled out his erection, revealing a long, slender cock, then stroked it as he watched Trey's big hand caress her breast.

Mia's gaze flicked back to the TV. Angela moved to number six—Mia had missed her finishing off number five—and the man who had been stroking her ass moved forward and pressed his long, condom-covered cock against her opening. As it slid inside Angela, Mia groaned, wanting to feel the same thing. As the man thrust into Angela again and again, Mia reached out with both hands, groping at the men beside her. She wrapped her fingers around Jake's naked cock above his hand. He moved out of the way and she stroked the length of his shaft from base to tip. His flesh was hot and hard in her hand.

At the same time, she ran her hand over Trey's impressive bulge. Trey guided her hand to his zipper and pulled it down for her. Jake stood up and shed his pants, then drew her hand back to his cock. Trey took her other hand and slipped it inside his pants and her fingers encircled his cock, too.

Angela wailed as the man continued to thrust into her, then moaned as both the man in her mouth and the one pumping her from behind groaned in climax. Mia's eyelids fluttered closed and she groaned at the sensation as Jake's mouth covered her nipple as her hands clutched tightly at the two sexy, hard cocks. Trey's hand trailed down her stomach, then over her belly. His fingers dipped under the elastic of her panties and between her legs, then found the wetness pooling there. She squeezed their cocks and pumped.

She opened her eyes and watched the screen in fascination as another man rolled on a condom and entered Angela, who now leaned back against the hot tub facing him. She clung to him as he thrust into her.

"Oh, God, one of you make love to me," Mia pleaded, needing relief from the desire burning through her.

Jake stood up, his cock tugging free from her hand. He leaned down and kissed her, sweet and lingering, then drew her panties down and off. He knelt in front of her and she felt his cock-head brush her slit, then ease forward.

"Yes, fuck me. Fuck me hard," Angela cried on the screen.

"Yeah, please," Mia echoed as Jake pushed into her. She wrapped her arms around him, pulling him close to her body.

Jake pulled back then eased forward again. Mia's body felt

heavy with need and her intimate muscles clenched around him. He sensed her eagerness and need for more. He pulled back and thrust forward again, then again.

Trey cupped Jake's balls with one hand and stroked her hair with the other as Jake thrust into her. Again and again. Heat burned through her and Angela's wail of climax burst through her, driving her pleasure higher. Jake stiffened, then pulsed inside her. She felt the heat of him flooding into her and she flew over the edge, wailing in release.

Jake held her tight to his body, then slowly released her. He slid free of her and Trey immediately slid inside. He spiraled, then thrust. An immediate swell of renewed pleasure consumed her. He thrust in and out. The pleasure built to a blissful state, then exploded in another orgasm. He erupted inside her.

As Mia fell back on the couch, fully sated, Angela cried out again, another man pumping into her. Mia just watched the screen in fascination, her limbs tangled with Jake and Trey, as Angela fucked each and every one of the young men. When they were all satisfied, they each kissed her with passion, then she bid them good night. Once they had all left, she winked at one camera, then shut them both off.

Harmony pulled her VIP card from her purse.

"Won't it be a tight squeeze for the whole group of us to have breakfast in one room?" Aiden asked.

"It's a three-bedroom suite with a full kitchen, dining

room, and living room." Harmony slid the card into the slot in the door. The light turned green and she turned the knob and opened the door. "There's plenty of room."

Bright sunlight and the murmur of voices greeted them. They stepped into a small entryway with a closet on one side. Harmony dropped her purse into the closet then walked down the hall, Aiden behind her. A living room with a huge window on one wall and a patio door on the adjacent wall stood on their left, and an open, airy kitchen on their right.

"There's Harmony and Aiden." Trey smiled at them from the kitchen. "Want a coffee?"

At Harmony's nod, he grabbed the glass pot from the coffeemaker on the counter and poured two cups. Aiden headed straight to his cup and added sugar and cream, then took a sip.

"That's what I needed." He settled on a stool next to the counter and picked up a slice of apple from a fruit tray sitting beside the coffee service.

Harmony added cream to her coffee and nibbled on a piece of pineapple. A wonderful sweet tanginess burst on her tongue. Trey and Nikki were in the kitchen and she noticed that Angela and Cole were in the living room. She strolled over to one of the armchairs and sat by Cole and Angela, who sat together on the couch. Large potted plants stood in various places around the room and Harmony could see sunlight glistening off the ocean outside the window.

"Did you and Trey and Jake have fun last night, Angie?" Harmony asked.

"Fabulous." She smiled broadly. "In fact, we made a new friend."

Harmony smiled. "You always make new friends."

"Yes, but we want to ask the rest of you if this friend can join the group for the vacation. I was just talking to Cole about it."

"That's right." Trey crossed the room and sat in the other armchair. "The four of us had a great time last night and she's here on her own and a bit lonely."

"The more the merrier." Nikki sat on the arm of Trey's chair. "Have you asked her to come this morning?"

"Yeah, Jake should be bringing her any minute now."

"Actually, Aiden, you know her already."

A sharp chill shot down Harmony's spine. The door lock beeped and pushed open, but Trey was blocking her view so she couldn't see who was there.

"That'll be them." Angela stood up and headed to the door, too.

"Come on in and meet the group. Everyone's here," Trey said.

"You're sure no one minds that I'm here?" a familiar female voice asked.

Aiden's head spun toward the door and he leapt to his feet.

Jake stepped farther into the room, past Angela and Trey, leading *Mia*. Aiden's ex, damn it!

"Mia?" Aiden glanced from her to Harmony.

Mia stopped in her tracks as soon as she saw Aiden. Her eyes widened.

"We figured this would work out well since you two already know each other."

"Oh, no, I didn't know Aiden was going to be here." Mia shook her head. "This is not a good idea."

"But you knew Aiden was with us," Angela said. "You saw him at dinner on Friday."

"I thought . . . When I asked, one of you said you'd just met him. I thought that meant he'd just joined your party for the evening . . . you know, someone you met on vacation. Sort of like you asked me to join you for dinner."

"We *had* just met Aiden," Jake said, "but he came here with Harmony, who is part of the group."

She turned to Aiden. "I'm sorry, I really didn't know. I didn't mean to intrude."

Harmony's chest clenched at the implications of this. If Mia was in the group, she was easily accessible to Aiden sexually. He could make love to her without guilt. The thought of it sent chills through Harmony. He had loved this woman, maybe still did. The situation couldn't get more awkward and upsetting.

"Mia, wait." Aiden strode toward the door, but Mia continued outside. Aiden glanced toward Harmony, his jaw set with determination, then strode after his ex-girlfriend. The door closed behind him with a thud.

Silence hung over the group for a few moments.

"I guess they don't have that kind of relationship," Nikki said.

"Oh, they have exactly that kind of relationship." Harmony picked up her coffee cup in a shaking hand and took a sip.

The others returned to the living room. Cole slipped out the sliding door to the private patio beyond. Harmony ate a slice of orange, not tasting it, then took another sip of coffee, trying not to think about Aiden chasing Mia down. Comforting Mia, while she sat here a nervous wreck.

Cole sat down beside her. "I saw them talking on the patio near the tennis courts, just down a ways to the left. If you go out the sliding door, you could catch up with them."

She glanced at him hesitantly. "I don't know."

He rested his hand on her arm. "You don't have to interrupt them. You could just see if everything's all right . . ."

She pushed herself to her feet and walked on numb legs to the door, then slid it open. The bright sunshine and warm salty air caressed her face as she stepped outside, closing the door behind her. She walked past the bushes, which offered the condo patio privacy, and opened the gate. She saw Mia sitting at a table under an umbrella about fifty yards away. Aiden sat across from her.

Not many people were around. This section was a private area, reserved for the guests with condos.

Harmony walked toward them, then hesitated several yards away near a tall, flowering plant. They were engrossed

in their conversation and didn't notice her. She didn't want
to hide from them, but she didn't want to interrupt either.

Aiden held Mia's hand.

"I'm surprised you got involved with them," he said.

"*You're* involved with them," Mia tossed back.

"I didn't mean it as an insult. I just meant that I find it
hard picturing you being free and easy sexually with people
you don't even know."

Harmony clenched her fists. *Unlike me.*

Mia stared down at their joined hands. "I know what you
mean, but . . . they aren't like strangers. They made me feel
welcome. Wanted. I'm very comfortable with them. They
really made me feel like I belong." She sighed. "But, don't
worry. I know I can't stay in the group. Not with you and
Harmony."

Harmony let out a sigh of relief, then waited for Aiden's
reaction.

"I hate to see you spend the week all alone. I know how
miserable that will make you." He squeezed her hand. "Let
me talk to Harmony. Maybe I can work something out with
her."

Harmony's gut clenched. Aiden wanted Mia in the group.
Harmony turned and fled.

FOURTEEN

Harmony sat on the wooden bench and stared at the waves as they surged onto the sand, then rolled back. People strolled along the boardwalk, passing her, oblivious to her heartache.

"Harmony, is everything all right?"

Harmony glanced around to see Cole behind her. He sat down beside her on the hard bench.

"What happened? Did you find Aiden and Mia?"

She nodded, then stared down at her hands. "I overheard them talking. I think Aiden's going to ask me to let Mia join the group."

Cole rested his elbows on his legs, his hands folded between his knees as he leaned forward and watched the waves. Bright sunlight glinted on the water as soft, wispy clouds floated in the vivid blue sky.

"What do *you* want?" Cole asked.

"I don't want her here."

"Good. So you've made your decision," Cole said.

Harmony's heart clenched as she remembered Mia's observations about the group.

They aren't like strangers. They made me feel welcome . . . like I belong.

She knew exactly what Mia meant. That's how she felt with the group.

"I feel like I'm being selfish."

He gently grasped her shoulders. "It's okay to want what you want." The comforting grip of his hands and the warmth in his gray eyes reassured her. "It's okay to put your own happiness first."

"The other group members want her here."

"They don't understand the situation. If they did—"

"Aiden wants her here." Her chest tightened.

"And why is that more important than what you want?"

"He's worried about her being here alone, with no friends."

Cole took her hand and brought it to his mouth. The brush of his lips on the back of her hand soothed her.

"She'll find friends. She doesn't have to have yours."

Talking to Cole had made Harmony feel better, but she still wasn't ready to face Aiden. She grabbed a taxi and went into town to do some sightseeing. When she returned to the resort, it was close to seven in the evening. She closed the door behind her and noticed the adjoining door was open.

"Harmony?" Aiden's head popped through the doorway. "There you are. I was wondering where you've been all day."

"I went into town sightseeing." She refused to feel guilty for not telling him where she'd gone, but she didn't like the defensive tone in her voice.

"Okay . . . I just wanted to talk to you about something."

Damn, here it comes. Harmony sat in one of the armchairs.

"You want Mia to join the group?" Her voice sounded strained.

"What? No, of course not." Aiden sat in the chair beside her.

"But you'd like her to be part of the group?"

He hesitated. "I just . . . hate to see her here all alone. I wanted to ask if there was any way she could spend a little time with the group, for a couple of meals or whatever, without ruining things."

Harmony tapped her fingers on her lap, unsure how to respond.

"It would be weird. If anyone wanted to start anything . . . with another person there . . ."

"I understand." He scratched his chin. "Well, she chose to come here alone. I guess she'll have to just deal with it."

Harmony's fingers curled around the arms of the chair.

"Aiden, did Mia come here to try to win you back?"

He hesitated. "She . . . wanted to let me know how she feels about me, but I've told her I'm with you now . . . that she and I are over. It's time to move on." He drew her hand to his mouth and kissed the back of her fingers, sending shivers through her. "Honey, please don't be jealous of Mia. It's *you* I want to be with."

She stared at him and her heart melted.

He loved her. She could see it in his eyes.

Damn. She had brought him here to test him by exposing him to the group and her activities, and he had passed with flying colors. He not only accepted how she behaved in the group, he applauded her uninhibited behavior.

The question now was, did he love Harmony more than Mia? What better way to find out than to give him the choice and see which one he picked. If he'd rather have Mia than Harmony then it would be better to find out now, before they got married.

Hoping to win Aiden by keeping him away from temptation certainly didn't seem like a sound course of action. There would always be temptation. The real measure of a man is what he does in the face of it.

She rested her hands on her knees and leaned forward.

"You know what, Aiden? I think it might be a good idea to have Mia as part of the group. Trey and Jake want her to join and we are short a woman."

Aiden stared at her skeptically.

"And what do you want?"

"I want to know that having her accessible won't change how you feel about me."

"Harmony, whatever I have to do to prove to you that I

love you, I'll do." He stood up and pulled her to her feet and into his arms. "As long as at the end of the week, you agree to marry me."

His mouth captured hers and all thoughts of Mia faded from her mind.

As Harmony rode the elevator down, all her insecurities swelled in a rush of chaos. What in hell had she been thinking inviting Mia to join the group? Sure, Aiden had promised to not make love to Mia, but . . .

She sucked in a deep breath. Aiden had asked her to marry him. He had reaffirmed that sentiment moments ago.

And that was the other thing that was bothering her. If she married Aiden, would she ever come to another group vacation? Aiden had agreed to come this one time, but what about the future?

This could be the last time she ever enjoyed a wild, exciting vacation with the infamous group of six. Her heart ached with a sense of loss. She loved these people. They were a very important part of her life. And her identity.

She strode across the stone path through the wide lawn leading to the parking lot.

"Harmony?"

She glanced up to see Jake standing a few yards away. He was wearing a nicely tailored dress jacket, yet he had a light shadow of stubble across his strong jawline, which made him look all the more sexy. His shoulder-length hair was tied back behind his head as always. Just knowing that wild mass of hair was tamed by one small elastic had her itching to tug it free.

"You okay?" he asked.

She curled her hand around his elbow and drew close.

"I want you," she murmured in his ear, then pressed close to his body.

"I'm meeting Nikki and Trey. Do you want to join us for the evening?"

"I want you now." She arched her body against his as she slid one arm around his neck and pulled his face to hers, then kissed him. Her tongue glided into his mouth as her hand stroked down his chest . . . over his stomach . . . lower . . . His cock rose under her hand.

His tongue tangled with hers and his arms surrounded her. He pulled her close, his cock grinding into the cradle of her pelvis. Not close enough to her burning center.

He drew his mouth from hers and glanced around.

"The limousine is just over there," he said. "It's waiting for Cole and Angela but I'm sure they won't mind if we use it. They were going to give us a lift into town."

He grabbed her hand and led her to the long elegant white vehicle. The chauffeur opened the door for them and Harmony slid inside, followed by Jake. As the door closed behind them, Jake sat down beside her. She slid her hand along Jake's thigh and stroked over the growing bulge under his fly. He unzipped his pants and popped open the hook. She slid into his briefs and grasped the steely rod of flesh. She drew him out and stroked several times. His cock was slender, but quite long.

"Mmm. You want me."

"You know it, doll."

She leaned down and licked his shaft, her tongue gliding over the veined surface, then she swallowed the tip. She bobbed up and down a couple of times.

He drew her back up, then knelt in front of her.

He pushed up her skirt and slid his hand over her mound, which was melting with heat. His fingers slid under her panties.

"Baby, you are so wet."

She slid her hands around his neck and pulled him to her lips. She drew his tongue into her mouth, then sucked on him deeply.

"Oh, now," she pleaded, needing him inside her.

He tugged her panties down and dropped them on the floor, then slid his fingers inside her and stroked. She arched against his hand. He lowered his head and she felt his tongue push between her folds and lick her.

"Oh, that's so good."

His tongue found her clit and pleasure spiked through her.

"I want you. Now. *Right now*."

He grabbed his cock and pushed it against her opening.

"Oh, yeah. Push it inside."

She could see the chauffeur's eyes in the mirror, discreetly watching them. Ordinarily, the audience, especially one as great looking as the blond, chisel-featured driver, would make her even hotter, but right now she just didn't care. She was too caught up in needing Jake to pay him any mind.

Jake pushed forward, his long cock impaling her. She wrapped her legs around his waist, pulling him in deeper.

"Do it. Fuck me hard," she insisted. The crude language fit her mood.

He drew back, then accelerated forward. Her head spun with the intense sensations. He thrust into her. Deep. Hard. Increasing in speed. Unnamed emotions roiled through her. Her desire built steadily with his thrusts . . . pleasure swirling through her. She gasped at his deep thrusts, her heartbeat pounding. She clung to him, waiting for the release of orgasm to encompass her. She squeezed his shoulders as she felt it build inside her.

He groaned and erupted inside her.

She hung onto him as his rigid body pulsed within her, then he relaxed and gazed at her face. He stroked the hair back from her face.

"I'm sorry, sweetheart. I thought you were with me."

"It's okay, I—"

"Excuse me," the driver said, no longer gazing in the mirror. "Another guest has arrived."

Harmony tugged her skirt down and Jake readjusted his pants.

Jake opened the door and when he saw Trey standing there, pulled him into the car.

"Harmony is horny as hell, man. I think she could use your help."

Harmony unfastened the buttons of her soft cotton shirt and pulled the sides open, revealing her lace-clad breasts. She flicked open the clasp and bared them to him.

"Okay. You not up to the job?" he asked Jake, a half-grin on his face.

"Hey, just give the lady what she wants," he said in a good-natured banter.

Trey stroked one of Harmony's nipples then leaned forward and sucked it into his mouth. The hot wet sensation sent her hormones fluttering. She unfastened his pants and grabbed his growing cock.

"She's really wet and ready," Jake prompted.

Trey's fingers found her naked mound and he stroked along her slit, dipping inside.

"You're right about that." He pushed his fingers in deeper and fluttered inside, then stroked the wall of her slick vagina. His thumb dabbed her clit and she arched forward at the intense stimulation.

Her fingers clenched around the lapels of his jacket.

"Fuck me, Trey. Fuck me hard."

Again she noticed the chauffeur's intense gaze in the mirror.

Trey shifted, placing his cock-head against her moistness, then he thrust forward. Jake continued to stroke her breast as Trey fucked her deep and hard. She gasped and moaned, feeling an orgasm close in on her.

"Yeah, baby. Fuck me. Make me come."

She gasped as he thrust deeper still.

Trey thrust three more times, then stiffened and exploded inside her. She clenched around him, gripping his pulsing cock with her vaginal muscles . . . . but still the orgasm didn't come.

She slumped back on the seat.

"Harmony . . ." Trey kissed her neck, then drew out. "I'm really sorry, honey."

"I know what she needs," Jake said as Trey fastened his pants again.

Harmony just stayed slumped on the seat, her naked breasts on full display to the driver. She felt a little sorry for him, probably extremely horny with no way to release his tension. She stroked one breast, giving him something to concentrate on.

Jake slid past Trey and Harmony and slipped out the door, ensuring Harmony couldn't be seen from outside.

"Is Nikki going to be showing up, too?" Harmony asked Trey.

"No, we were going to drive over to pick her up. You know, treat it like a date."

"With two such handsome men. How lovely," said Harmony.

The car started to move and Harmony noticed Jake outside, walking along one of the stone paths to the hotel, talking on his cell phone. The car stopped a few moments later.

Harmony buttoned up her blouse and straightened her skirt once again.

A few moments later, Jake approached with Cole and Angela alongside him.

Jake stuck his head in the car.

"I thought Cole might be able to help you, Harmony."

Cole stuck his head in the car, too, with a big grin.

She smiled. Cole was just what she needed and she was lucky to be part of a group of people who were so caring.

What would she do without the infamous group of six?

After Nikki, Jake, and Trey decided to take a taxi into town, Cole climbed in the back with Harmony. Angela smiled at the driver.

"How about I ride up front with you?" Angela suggested.

"I'm sorry, ma'am. That's against the rules," he said in a delightful French accent. He did look sorry, too.

Angela stroked a finger along his tie.

"I won't tell if you won't." She glanced around and, ensuring no one was looking, took his hand and brought it to her breast. "Why don't you take us somewhere romantic and secluded? Maybe a nice beach?"

"I know just the place," he said as he started up the car and lurched forward.

"How are you doing?" Cole asked as his arm went around Harmony's shoulders. "I heard you were having some problems? The guys couldn't finish the job, and that's not like them. Or you."

"I know. It's not their fault. I've just had a lot on my mind. I told Aiden we should let Mia into the group. I de-cided if he really loves me, there should be no problem. And if there is a problem, it's better to find out now."

"Wow. I can see why you're out of sorts. Agreeing to let your fiancé's ex-girlfriend have sex in front of him, and prob-ably with him, will do that to a person."

"He's not my fiancé."

He smiled. "I see." He eased closer and captured her mouth with his. The gentle pressure, then the feel of his tongue gliding along the seam of her lips made her melt. She opened for him and his tongue slid inside to tangle with hers.

"So, you mean, there's still hope for me?" he asked.

She drew back and met his simmering charcoal gaze.

FIFTEEN

Harmony wanted to ask Cole what he meant, but the car took a sharp turn and drove down a winding road, then pulled to a stop a moment later.

The driver opened their door. "There are blankets in the trunk. And a cooler with champagne and hors d'oeuvres."

Harmony glanced at the lovely stretch of moonlit beach. There were cliffs around them, blocking the road from view.

Cole got out and held out his hand to help her from the car. He tucked a blanket over his arm and held her hand as they walked along the beach. Angela slipped out of the front seat and sat on the side of the hood.

The driver watched her as he pulled the cooler from the trunk and strode after Harmony and Cole. Cole handed Harmony the blanket and took the cooler from the driver.

"You go enjoy yourself." He nodded toward Angela and the driver smiled, then turned around.

Harmony headed to a large rock alone in the sea of sand. Cole placed the cooler on the sand, then spread the blanket at the base of the rock.

Harmony glanced back at the car and saw Angela pull a condom from her bag as the driver ensconced himself between Angela's legs.

Cole laid Harmony down on the blanket and drew her blouse from her shoulders, followed by her unfastened bra, then tossed them aside. He tucked his hand under the small of her back and lifted a little, then unfastened her skirt button and zipper, then rested her back on the ground and slipped the skirt downward and off.

He grinned as his gaze wandered the length of her totally naked body.

"You seem to have lost something."

Her panties. They were on the floor of the limousine. She'd better remember to pick those up or the next clients would get a bit of a thrill.

Cole stroked her body from shoulder to calf, thrilling her senses.

"You are so beautiful, dream girl." He nuzzled her neck, then kissed down her breastbone in whisper-soft brushes of his lips. "And sweet and smart and fun to be with." He smiled at her with dark, simmering eyes. "When I finally settle down, I'd like it to be with someone just like you."

Despite his light tone, the intensity of his gaze bored through her. She drew in a breath and forced a smile.

"You? Settle down? I bet you're too busy with a lineup of sexy women just waiting their turn."

He stroked his finger down her stomach. His tender touch sent a quiver through her.

"For a long time it has suited me to have relationships that have no commitments. Mainly because of what I have here with the group . . ." The moonlight glimmered in his charcoal eyes. "With you . . ." He lifted her hand and stroked her palm with his lips. "Every year, I look forward to seeing you, being with you . . . After our vacations, I return home and spend time working to build my business, knowing one day, I want to settle down with the woman of my dreams and have a family." He stroked her cheek. "I just hope that it's not too late."

She simply stared at him with wide eyes. Could he mean that . . . ?

His mouth covered her nipple and she sucked in a lungful of the salty ocean air.

He kissed and nuzzled, then suckled each of her nipples until they ached with need. Then he began another downward progression. When his mouth covered her clit, she was desperate with need. His tongued dabbed, then licked her. She clung to his head, his dark waves coiling around her fingers as she forked them through his hair.

He sucked her clit lightly, bringing her close to the edge, then eased off. Then suckled again. She pulled him tighter against her body, needing him closer.

He dabbed and teased, bringing her close many times.

At the sound of gasps and groans, Harmony glanced toward the car. Angela leaned forward, her hands propped on the hood of the car while the driver thrust into her from behind. He pounded in and out.

"Oh, yeah, baby. That's so good." Angela's voice caught, then she wailed in release.

The driver groaned and stiffened, clearly coming right along with her.

Cole sucked again and the clouds of bliss plumed to an immediate and intense orgasm, pulsing through every part of her.

"Oh, heavens," she gasped as she flopped on the blanket, her arms spread wide. "You are amazing."

"I can't take all the credit. You were pretty well primed by Jake and Trey." He rested his elbow on the blanket beside her and rested his head on his hand. "And the show Angela is putting on over there certainly didn't hurt."

She grasped his cheeks and pulled his face to hers, then kissed him soundly on the lips. "That may be, but it was you who succeeded." She kissed him again, and rolled him over until she was slanted across his body. "All you."

She tangled her fingers in his shirt and unfastened his buttons, her fingers gliding along hard muscle as she moved downward. Her lips captured his again and his hand stroked over her naked buttocks.

"Poor Cole. We've all made the mark and he's still wanting." A naked Angela flopped down on the blanket beside them and began unfastening Cole's belt.

The chauffeur stood behind her, wearing a pair of black boxers, until Harmony smiled at him. He settled on the blanket behind Angela as she unzipped Cole's fly.

"Oh, this is André. He's a university student from France—actually graduated last year—and he's working here for a year before he starts his post-graduate studies next September," Angela explained.

When had Angela found all that out? They'd seemed too busy to chat.

Harmony rolled onto her side, facing Angela and André.

"Hi, André. Nice to meet you."

He smiled and his eyes simmered with interest as his gaze glided over her naked breasts, then to her face.

"Thank you. You also." His gaze shifted to her breasts again.

She smiled and drew her fingers over her nipple—to tease him, and because of the exciting tingle his hot gaze triggered.

Angela drew Cole's hard cock from his pants and licked the tip.

"You know, André has never tried anal sex," she mentioned. "Nor ménage à trios. Which seems an awful shame, since he is French and the term is in French and . . ." She grinned at Harmony. "I thought maybe if you were game . . ." She nudged Harmony. "You could do the first with him and I'll do the second. With Cole's help, of course."

Harmony gazed at André's face. Neat, streamlined features, full lips, and a boyish glint in his eyes made his face charmingly handsome.

She smiled. "I think I could be convinced."

Angela released Cole's cock and handed André a condom. Harmony wrapped her fingers around Cole's cock and glided up and down. It felt like hot, hard steel. Harmony leaned forward and swallowed his cock-head into her mouth, pushing her behind in the air.

André stroked over the curve of her ass, then glided forward and around to cup her breasts. Harmony dove deeper on Cole's cock, swallowing him all the way.

"Honey," Angela said, "slide your cock into her pussy for lubrication, then go for it. Slowly."

André's hands released Harmony's breasts and she heard him shuffle around behind her, probably removing his boxers, then she felt him kneel close behind her again. Hard flesh nudged her opening, then his cock slid into her. At the hot, hard invasion, she gripped him inside her. He glided forward and back a few strokes, then pulled out again. A moment later, he nudged her back opening. She sucked on Cole as the cock behind her eased forward. Slowly. She squeezed against him and his cock-head slipped inside.

"That's good, honey," Angela encouraged. "Keep going."

"Oh, it is so tight. It is amazing," he said.

Then he was all the way in. Angela grabbed one of the pillows and slid underneath Harmony and licked her nipple. Both her nipples hardened at the stimulation of Angela's gentle nuzzling. As André pulled back, slowly caressing her tight passage, Angela's hand stroked down Harmony's stomach, then her finger nudged between Harmony's legs.

André pushed in again and Harmony sucked on Cole's cock, squeezing him within her mouth.

"C'est étonnant," André uttered on a hard breath.

Angela slid another finger into Harmony's slit and glided in and out. That and the hot hard feel of André pumping her from behind sent heat flooding through Harmony. She sucked Cole harder.

André tensed and groaned. She felt his cock pulse inside her ass. Cole tensed and hot liquid erupted into her mouth. Angela tweaked Harmony's clit, but it was not enough.

She released Cole's spent cock.

"It's okay, Angie. I'm good for now."

And she was. She wanted to wait for Cole's cock to make her come again.

Angela shifted from under Harmony with a sheepish grin.

"Okay, sweetie. If you're sure."

"Now it's time for your ménage."

"Except that you've used them all up." Angela winked.

"I know how to get them going again." Harmony grabbed Angela's wrists and forced her down to the blanket, then held her wrists to the side of her head as she prowled over her. Angela pretended to struggle against her.

"What are you doing? Let me up." Angela's words, filled with mock anxiety, made Harmony grin.

She leaned down and lapped at one of Angela's large nipples. The aureole pebbled under her tongue and the nipple distended into a hard nub. Harmony circled her tongue around and around the bead of flesh.

"Oh, yes . . . I mean no," Angela wailed.

Harmony leaned forward and captured Angela's mouth. She knew men got wildly turned on by seeing two women kiss. She pushed her tongue into Angela's soft mouth. Her tongue met Harmony's and they tangled together as their lips played on each other's. Harmony drew back and sucked Angela's other nipple into her mouth.

She glanced at the men, both watching intently. She nudged her head toward Angela's left hand and Cole immediately moved forward and took Angela's wrist and held it down. André followed suit and captured Angela's right wrist. The two men leaned forward and lapped and sucked Angie's nipples as Harmony parted her thighs and kissed below her navel, then parted her folds until she could see the small nub of flesh buried there. She leaned forward and licked her clit. Angela moaned loudly.

Harmony noticed that both men's cocks were at full attention.

"I'll leave this to you two men now," Harmony said as she moved back and found a comfortable place on the edge of the blanket, propped against a pillow to watch.

Cole grabbed Angela's wrist from André and drew her forward. He kissed her, long and hard.

"Sit," Harmony whispered to André.

He glanced at her, then sat down on the blanket, his legs sprawled out in front of him. She handed him a new condom from Angela's open bag and he rolled it on. Cole eased Angela backward until she was crouched over André. André pressed his cock against her hovering vagina and dipped in a couple of times, then shifted his cock to her back opening and nudged against her. Cole lowered her down.

"Oh, honey." Angela clamped her hands around André's thighs.

"Did you want front or back," Cole asked. "Because we can switch."

"No, this is *fantasique*," André said.

Cole nodded, then wrapped his arms around Angela and drew her forward as he rolled back, pulling her on top of him. André's cock dropped free. Cole's cock impaled her. She now sat atop Cole, his cock deep inside her. She leaned forward and offered her ass to André again. He pushed himself forward and crouched behind her, then eased his cock into her once again.

Angela pushed herself up, then down on Cole's cock. Harmony could imagine the two male members inside her, the intense feeling of fullness, the heat of their two bodies sandwiching hers.

Angela moaned in pleasure. "You two guys are too much."

"Too much?" André looked startled. "Should I stop?"

"It's just an expression, André," Harmony assured.

His tense features relaxed into a smile and he nodded.

Cole pivoted his hips up and down, pushing his cock into her in small thrusts while André hung onto her hips and pulsed in and out of her in an increasing rhythm. Angela bounced up and down, taking their two cocks deep and hard.

The three bodies moved in unison, as the men pumped into Angela in a heated dance of passion. Her moans of pleasure increased, becoming more frenzied as they raced toward orgasm.

"I'm coming. Oh, God, I'm coming . . ." Angela whimpered, then her words trailed off into a wail of pleasure.

The men continued to pump into her. First André groaned his release, then Cole.

The three of them sat there for a few moments, catching their breath. Harmony definitely needed some cooling off.

"Come on, you guys. I want to go skinny-dipping." Harmony pushed herself to her feet and raced toward the water. The full moon sparkled on the rippling waves.

The other three separated, then followed her. She ran into the water. It was cool against her feet and she stopped ankle-deep, then leaned over and splashed the others.

Cole scooped her up and raced into the water with her, then tossed her into the waves. She cried out as the cool water surrounded her, then she went under. She hit the soft sandy bottom and pushed herself to her feet.

"You're going to pay for that," she threatened as she raced straight toward him, then leaped into his arms. He caught her and held her tight to his body. She wrapped her arms and legs around him.

"If this is punishment, bring it on."

She could feel his cock hardening against her hot, slippery slit, which was pressed up against his belly.

She kissed him hard and long, pushing her tongue between his lips to explore the inner depths. He kissed her back, with just as much exuberance. She could hear André and Angela splashing around in the ocean behind her.

His cock nudged against her. It was hot and hard and it triggered an ache deep inside her.

He kissed her with a passion that took her breath away.

"I want you, Harmony." The intense glow in his eyes made her think he meant more than wanting a quick fuck in the ocean.

His cock nudged her slit, then it drove into her. Deep and hard. Filling her. Stroking her. He cupped her buttocks, then pulled back and thrust forward again.

"Oh, Cole." She clung to his strong shoulders and tightened her legs around him.

The ocean waves pulsed against them. Cole's strong arms held her close, keeping her snug against his body.

He thrust again and she felt it. That intense longing . . . then a powerful pleasure building in her body, flooding through her cells. His cock thrust into her again, making her gasp. She arched against him, trying to pull him in deeper.

He thrust harder and faster. She sucked in air, her breaths

becoming gasps, as she rose on an ever-increasing cloud of bliss.

"Come for me, honey. I want to see your beautiful face, like an angel's, as I take you to heaven."

His fast, deep thrusts carried her away. Pleasure rushed through her and she gasped as she burst into ecstasy.

"Yes, sweetheart. Oh, God, you're so beautiful." He groaned and she felt his hot, liquid release.

As she stared at his simmering charcoal eyes, he stroked her cheeks with an aching tenderness.

"I love you, Harmony," he murmured against her ear.

Shock catapulted through her and she drew in a deep breath.

Oh, God, what should she say?

"Hey, you two. Why don't we check out that picnic basket?"

At Angela's voice, Cole eased back. His cock pulled free and cool water swirled around her, erasing the feel of his hot, hard body against hers. He kissed Harmony, then smiled as he offered her a hand. She took it and followed him as they raced toward the beach.

Harmony saw the lights glowing from the tall tower of the resort as André passed a clump of palm trees, then turned right onto the road leading to Hidden Paradise. He stopped in front of the main building. Angela gave him a long, ardent kiss, then he smiled at her as if he didn't want her to leave.

Harmony smiled. They certainly made an attractive couple. André kissed Angela again, then exited the limousine and walked around to open her door. She stood up and smoothed down her skirt, then André opened the back door and Harmony took his offered hand as she stepped out of the vehicle. Cole followed her out.

"Thank you. It was a lovely evening," Angela said as if nothing out of the ordinary had occurred between her and the handsome chauffeur.

"If you need a driver again during your time here, please give me a call," he said in his sexy French accent and he handed her a card.

Harmony noticed he'd written a number on it in pen in addition to the company number. Probably his personal cell phone number.

"I will," Angela said with a glint in her eye.

Harmony and Cole bid good-bye to André, then Cole took Harmony's arm. They walked up the steps to the hotel entrance and the glass doors slid open.

"Your place or mine?" Cole asked.

"Oh, Harmony's place," Angela said, falling into step beside them as they crossed the lobby. "Maybe Aiden will be in."

SIXTEEN

Harmony hooked her arm around Cole's. She doubted Aiden would be sitting around in the room. She didn't even want to think about where he was, especially since every one in the group had had plans—other than Aiden . . . and Mia.

Angela linked arms with Cole and he escorted both of them to the elevator. Harmony was just as happy to have Angela along after the bombshell Cole had dropped. Angela pushed the elevator button.

Cole had told Harmony he loved her. Men sometimes did that in the throes of passion, but Cole had never done it before—not in twelve years. The fact that he'd done it tonight . . . the way he'd gazed at her with the moonlight glimmering in his eyes . . . so serious.

You are so beautiful . . . And sweet and smart and fun to be with . . . one day, I want to settle down with the woman of my dreams and have a family.

Someone just like you, he'd said. Is that why he'd always called her dream girl?

He'd never opened up to her like that before. The question racing through her mind was, did he really love her, or was he just wanting something he now knew he couldn't have . . . because of Aiden?

The thought that Cole might really be in love with her threw her into a maelstrom of confusion.

She loved Aiden, and Aiden had asked her to marry him. But she'd always had a special bond with Cole. He had been an important part of her life at college. They'd studied together, partied together, helped each other through break-ups. She could talk to him about anything, and he always encouraged her. That had continued through the years since college, too.

Could what she had with Cole be love? And if it was, what was she going to do? She couldn't have both men.

The elevator arrived and they stepped inside, followed by three other people in casual attire. Harmony pressed the button labelled fourteen and watched the view outside the glass wall of the elevator as they went up. Lights glittered in the distance and the moon cast a soft glow across the ocean waves.

The doors parted and Harmony opened her purse and rifled through it for the key card as the three of them strolled down the hall. Once inside the room, she tossed her purse on the dresser. The door to Aiden's adjoining room was closed.

"I wonder if he's there." Angela leaned her ear against the

door. "I think I hear someone in there." She paused, listening intently. "Jake, I think, and . . . a woman." She glanced over her shoulder at Harmony and Cole. "I think it might be that new woman, Mia. You know, I really like her. When she was with us last night . . ."

Angela kept talking, but Harmony couldn't concentrate enough to make sense of her words.

Aiden was in there with Mia? Was he having sex with her?

I'm such an idiot. I never should have suggested Mia join the group.

Cole's arm went around Harmony's waist and he pulled her to his side.

"Sweetheart, why don't you come back and stay in my room tonight?" Cole murmured against her ear.

Her spine stiffened at the thought of spending the night with Cole, of having to confront his feelings for her. She really couldn't handle that tonight.

Angela glanced at them. Her eyes narrowed and Harmony knew she'd figured out something was wrong.

"Actually, Cole, Harmony looks pretty tired." She glanced at Harmony as if seeking confirmation. Harmony nodded. "Why don't you and I go get a drink and see who's around?"

"I do feel like turning in now," Harmony said.

And it was true. Even though it was only nine thirty, all she wanted to do was climb into bed—alone—and go to sleep.

Cole's arms lingered around Harmony's waist.

"You sure?"

She nodded, then kissed him.

Angie took Cole's hand and led him toward the door. It closed quietly behind them.

Harmony took a quick shower then climbed into bed. As she lay snuggled under the covers, she listened intently, straining to hear any sounds coming from Aiden's room, but she heard nothing.

It was silly. She didn't even know if Mia was over there at all, let alone if Aiden was making love to her. She'd suggested Mia join the group to test the strength of Harmony and Aiden's relationship, and now she saw that there was a major flaw . . . and it was Harmony's. She didn't trust Aiden. She shouldn't be jumping to conclusions about him. He said he loved her. Why would he endanger that by having sex with Mia?

She heard a door open and close and voices in the hall-way. She sat upright. That was Mia's voice. And Aiden's. A moment later, Trey's joined in. She couldn't make out what they were saying—their voices were just murmurs—but she could tell they were getting closer.

A knock sounded at her door. She froze. Did they want to come in? Invite her to join them in a foursome?

The three of them had been in Aiden's room. Together. Probably having sex.

She felt sick to her stomach.

Another knock. She pulled the covers over her head, praying they would just go away.

The murmurs continued for a few more moments, then

drifted down the hall. Aiden's door closed. He must have stayed behind.

Part of her wanted to leap up, race over and confront him . . . but the rest of her sagged into her pillow. She was too exhausted. Anyway, what could she say? She'd been the one to suggest Mia join the group, and they'd been doing what the group did best.

For hours, she tossed and turned in bed, until the sheets twisted around her like giant vines. She dozed for a little while. When the first glimmer of dawn peered in her window, she pushed herself from the bed and got dressed, then headed downstairs for a walk on the beach.

Aiden stripped off his bathing trunks and tossed them over the edge of the bathtub, then climbed into the shower to wash off the salt from the pool water. Once he'd dried off, he padded into the bedroom, pulled on a pair of shorts, then strolled onto the balcony and stretched out on one of the lounge chairs.

The sound of the ocean waves washing on the beach combined with the sounds of people laughing and shouting during a lively game of beach volleyball. The clear blue sky was totally cloudless and the hot sun beat down on him, warming his skin.

This morning, he'd woken up to a red light flashing on his phone. Harmony had left a message to tell him the four women had gone into town shopping. Since he knew Harmony would be gone until the afternoon, he'd filled his time by taking a walk around the resort, playing a little tennis followed by a swim, then he'd had a late lunch by the pool.

He hoped Harmony would be back soon. He missed her. He hadn't seen her since she'd suggested Mia join the group yesterday evening. He wished Harmony had come to him last night.

He didn't know how late she'd been out. He never heard her come in. Trey and Mia had knocked on her door at about nine, but she hadn't answered. He'd come out to see who it was and invited them in for a drink. Mia had suggested they come by and thank Harmony for inviting her to join the group. Mia and Trey seemed to have hit it off, and Aiden was glad about that.

He shook his head. Damn, he wished Mia hadn't shown up here. Even though things seemed to be sorting themselves out, he shouldn't have allowed himself to get entangled with her again. His damned protective urges toward her had complicated things way too much. He loved Harmony and he didn't want to endanger their relationship for anything. His fists clenched in his lap. He would do whatever he could to show Harmony how much he loved her. Somehow, he would convince her to marry him.

He heard the door in the other room open. Harmony must be back.

He stood up and opened the sliding screen door, then poked his head through the adjoining doorway.

"Oh, hi." Harmony dropped some bags on the bed.

He stepped into her room.

She looked gorgeous in a red outfit that set off her dark hair beautifully. Actually, she wore her red bathing suit—which was his favorite because of the plunging neckline which revealed the swell of her breasts in a very enticing manner—with a wraparound skirt.

"Hi. I've been waiting for you." He stepped toward her, wanting to hug her, but she picked up a bag, pulled out a blouse, and held it up in front of her.

"Like it?"

It was emerald green and suited her beautifully, bringing out the green of her eyes.

"Nice."

She folded the garment and put it in the second drawer of the dresser. He stepped closer to her, but she swung around and grabbed another bag.

"I got something for you, too." She handed him a bigger bag than the one for her blouse.

He peered inside and pulled out a large beach towel with an abstract pattern of reds and oranges. It was a soft velour type and big enough to throw down on the beach and stretch out without having his feet hang over the end onto the sand.

"It's great. Thanks."

"I . . . thought it would be something to remind you of this trip."

He smiled. "I don't think I'll need reminding. This trip is *very* memorable."

"Well, then . . ." She glanced away, then grabbed another bag. "Something to remind you of me."

What the hell . . . ?

He took the bag from her hand and pulled her close, wrapping his arms around her. Her arms slid around his waist and she rested her head against his shoulder.

"Why would I need anything to remind me of you? You haven't decided to turn down my proposal, have you?"

"It's not that. I . . ."

She withdrew and sat on the edge of the bed, one knee tucked under her. She patted the bed beside her and he sank down. She took his hand.

"Last night, I . . . I was in bed and I heard Mia in the hall . . . she'd just come from your room."

"You were here? Why didn't you answer the door? Were you trying to sleep?"

She nodded.

He stroked her cheek. "I'm sorry, honey. Mia and Trey came over for a drink—I didn't mean to wake you up."

"Aiden, I know how much you loved Mia. And I know that she broke up with you. It would be only natural that, now that she wants you back . . . that you might be having second thoughts about . . . well, about us."

"I'm not having second thoughts."

She bit her lower lip and stared at him with glistening eyes. "Well, maybe you should be."

"I beg your pardon?"

"It's not that I don't want you." She drew his hand closer

to her and placed her other hand over it. "I just . . . I think
it's important that you at least consider your feelings for
Mia. I wouldn't want us to wind up married, then have you
always wonder what might have been."

He squeezed her hand, then brought it to his lips and
kissed it.

"Sweetheart, if you agree to marry me, I will never wonder about 'what if's'. Because I'll have you. And that's what I
want more than anything else."

"So you have no feelings at all left for Mia?"

He hesitated, but her solid stare told him he couldn't
dodge her question.

"I didn't say that."

Damn it. At her hurt expression, he felt guilty, but what
else could he say? He couldn't lie to her.

She stood up, but he tugged her back and into his arms.

"I love you, Harmony. I want to marry you."

He kissed her, his lips insistent. His tongue slid between
her lips and tangled with her tongue in an erotic dance. His
groin tightened at the feel of her soft mouth surrounding
him, her breasts pressing into his bare chest, her nipples
hardening into beads. At the evidence of her arousal, his cock
hardened, too.

"It's *you* I want, Harmony."

Her fingers raked through his hair and she tugged his face
back to her own. Her tongue invaded his mouth in a hot,
hungry dance. She slid one hand to his back and pulled him
tighter to her body, arching her breasts hard into his chest as

she stroked the back of his head with her other hand. Her mouth devoured his.

"I want you, too, Aiden." Her hand stroked down his chest and over his stomach. Then it reached the bulge in his shorts. She stroked over him once. His balls tightened in anticipation. She slid his zipper down and, a second later, her fingers encircled his cock.

At the feel of Aiden's hot, hard cock in her hand, Harmony felt a rush of heat between her legs.

She wanted him. Intensely.

She stood up and unwrapped her sarong, then peeled off her bathing suit. She stepped forward and stood before him, naked. He stood up and dropped his shorts to the floor, then dragged her back into his arms. His mouth invaded hers with hungry anticipation. She ran her hands over his tight buttocks and pulled his groin tightly to hers.

"Make love to me, Aiden. Right now."

He moved a hand down her stomach then a finger slid between her legs and dipped into her.

"You are so wet."

Although she'd asked for fast, Aiden wanted to give her more. He scooped her up and carried her to the side of the bed, then laid her down. He sat beside her and captured her lips with his, kissing her with a passion that flared deep from his heart.

"Honey, I love you so much." Aiden pressed her legs open, then knelt between them. "I want to make you feel so good."

He kissed her belly, then dipped his tongue into her navel. He stroked her hips as he kissed downward. Her soft, black curls teased his chin. He kissed around them, then down her inner thigh. She squirmed as he teased her, lifting her leg and kissing the back of her knees, then shifting to her other leg and kissing up her inner thigh.

Finally, as she arched toward him, her fingers tangling in his hair, he dabbed his tongue against her clit. A deep satisfaction burst through him at her strangled moan.

He flicked his tongue against her clit, then licked the length of her damp slit. She pulled his head tighter against her. He slid his tongue inside her, lapping deeply into her sweet pussy, then he shifted to her clit and sucked. She moaned and arched. He slid a finger into her hot, silky passage as he teased her clit with his tongue. Then he slid another finger inside. She arched again and her body tensed. She was close.

He stroked her vagina, finding the slightly bumpy part—her G-spot. She arched and moaned again, then wailed long and hard as dampness flooded from her.

Harmony pushed her hair back off her face as she slumped back on the bed. Her heart swelled at the way he had made her feel . . . cherished.

"My God, Aiden, that was incredible."

He grinned up at her.

"So you all done now?"

She clamped her hands around his shoulders.

"No way. Get up here, you fantastic hunk."

He prowled over her, his solid cock pointing toward her. He leaned down and sucked one nipple. She gasped at the exquisite pleasure. He sucked the other and she grabbed his shoulders and pulled him toward her. Their mouths met as his cock pressed against her moist folds.

She wanted him inside her. She needed to *feel* just how much he wanted her.

His cock glided into her and she sighed in pleasure. Clinging to his shoulders, she arched against him. He drew back and thrust forward.

Pleasure rose within her. She wrapped her legs around him. His cock thrust in deeper.

"Yes, Aiden. Make me come."

He thrust again, then spiraled out, then in again, increasing the intensity of her need. Her pulse pounded, then heat flooded through her as his thrusts increased. Deep. Hard. Intense pleasure burst through every cell, pulsing within her and through her, plummeting her into ecstasy.

He kept pumping, then joined her with his own release.

"Harmony, you look like a total slut." Aiden grinned at her as he leaned against the dresser, his arms crossed. "I love it."

Harmony finished fastening the tiny buckle on her strappy black leather shoe adorned with silver studs, then pushed herself to her feet, carefully balancing on the slender, silver-metal five-inch stiletto heels.

She glanced in the mirror and adjusted the form-fitting

red-and-black leather bustier which pushed her breasts up in an enticing manner. It left her midriff bare above her extremely short black leather skirt, which didn't manage to cover the tops of her stockings nor the black lace garters trimmed with red holding them up. When she walked, a glimpse of white thigh showed above the stockings.

"That's the idea. I'm fulfilling Jake's fantasy of having me be a hooker for him." Of course, it wouldn't be that straightforward. It never was. That's why these vacations were always so exciting. She tingled in anticipation.

Aiden slid his hands around her naked waist and nuzzled her neck.

"He's a very lucky man."

Harmony toyed with Aiden's collar and gazed into his warm brown eyes.

"You know, I can be your hooker when I get back later."

"Come on, don't kid yourself. You won't be back tonight and you know it."

"But if you want me to . . ."

"No, I don't want to cramp your style. This is your vacation. I want you to enjoy yourself, without worrying about me."

She grinned. "You have plans, too, don't you?"

The thought that it might be with Mia burned through her, but she pushed it aside. He had made a convincing argument that he still wanted to marry Harmony, despite his lingering feelings for Mia. Trust was an integral part of a relationship . . . and she trusted Aiden.

She slid her arms around his neck and kissed him. Long and hard.

"I'm going to miss you."

"No you won't," he teased. "You'll see." Then he patted her bottom and sent her toward the door. "Now get moving or you'll be late for your john."

"If I didn't know better, I'd say you're trying to get rid of me."

"Not at all," he said as he pulled open the door. "Now go."

A man walked down the corridor as she stepped into the hall in her skimpy hooker outfit.

Aiden grinned and said, "That was fabulous, Kiki. If you're free tomorrow night maybe you can stop by again."

He closed the door behind her. The stranger's eyebrow quirked up and he smiled at her.

"I'm looking for a little company if you're available," the man said, his gray eyes glinting as his gaze glided up and down her body, resting on the swell of her breasts pushed upward by the form-fitting bustier.

SEVENTEEN

All Harmony had to do was pull down the zipper on the tight garment to release her breasts to the stranger's view. Her fingers toyed with the tag of the zipper. The man's gaze remained locked on the swell of her breasts.

At the avid interest in his eyes, she was tempted. He was handsome and sexy and he wanted her—and that turned her on.

But she had to get to the suite where she was to meet Jake. He'd be waiting for her and tonight was about fulfilling Jake's fantasy, not this stranger's. Or her own.

She slid her hands over her breasts and winked. Maybe another evening this week, she could play the hooker again.

"Sorry, I'm already booked," she said, then strolled down the hall with an exaggerated wiggle which, from the burning feel of his hot gaze, he enjoyed.

An elevator ride and two right turns later, she stood outside the door to the suite and knocked.

"Come in."

She turned the doorknob and stepped inside.

"Sexy." Jake stared at her appreciatively. "Come here."

She closed the door and stepped in front of him. He wore faded blue jeans and a black T-shirt in soft cotton. His shoulder-length, light brown hair was a mass of waves around his face, rather than tied behind his head as usual. Sometimes he did that as part of the role-playing. She longed to reach out and stroke his whisker-shadowed jaw. He looked so raw and sexy.

He grasped the tag of her zipper and drew it down slowly. The tight leather encasing her chest released a little at a time. He peeled the fabric aside, baring her breasts. The style of the bustier included a collar—halter style—so when the zipper released, it hung open but did not fall off.

"Oh, yeah." He leaned in and sucked one nipple into his hot mouth. "You are one hot hooker."

He sucked hard, then nibbled on her other nipple.

"I want you to entertain me and my friend."

Someone stepped up behind her and stroked her ribs. The man's hand grazed over her nipple while Jake sucked on the other one. It was Trey behind her. She could tell by the way he rolled her nipple between his middle finger and thumb. Not the index finger like Cole and Jake did. His hand slid down her stomach, then slipped under her short, black leather skirt to glide over her panties. She could feel the moisture collecting between her legs.

"Wait. I'd like her to get us in the mood," Jake said.

Smiling, she stood up. "What would you like, honey?"

"I'd like a lap dance."

She turned her back to him and zipped up her top. She needed clothes on to do a striptease. She pulled a CD from her bag and crossed the room to the stereo and slipped the disc inside, then started the sultry music. She began to rotate her hips while doing a slow shoulder shimmy. She grabbed the chair from the desk and pulled it to the center of the floor, then turned her back on the two men, both now seated on the couch, and leaned forward, sliding up the hem of her skirt enough to give them a great view of her naked behind—at least, it might as well have been naked for all the G-string covered.

She stood up, swirling her hips around and around again as she drew down the zipper of her skirt, then dropped it to the ground and stepped out of it. She tossed a glance over her shoulder to see the men pulling out their cocks as she lowered herself over the seat of the chair, her legs wide open, her ass brushing the seat left to right. She pushed herself to her feet again, then dipped her ass down, then upward to the left, down, then upward to the right. She kicked one leg over the back of the chair and spun around to sit on the chair, her legs wide apart. She stroked her hand up her thigh, then over her crotch. The men's eyes glazed as they watched her fingers glide the length of her slit and back again. Jake reached for Trey's cock and stroked it along with his own. Trey reached for Jake's balls and cupped them in his hand.

She smiled and slid so that her legs pointed upward in a

straight line, her thighs resting on the chair back. Slowly, she tugged on the zipper pull, baring herself completely except for the G-string.

The men pumped faster as she opened her legs in a wide V. She ran her fingers down her thigh and over her slit again, feeling the wetness drenching her panties.

She rolled forward, her legs wide open, then lifted one leg straight up and over the back of the chair, then pushed herself to her feet.

In a sexy forward stride, she approached Jake, grabbed a handful of shirt and pulled him to his feet, then guided him to the chair. She turned it to face away from Trey, then sat Jake down with a push on his chest. She tucked his hot cock back in his pants and zipped him up, then she sat on his lap, facing Trey and she winked at him. She arched her body, pushing her pelvis against Jake and gyrating her hips. Around and around, pressing tight against his rock-hard cock. She pushed her breast against Jake's lips and he swallowed her nipple into his mouth. He suckled as she rocked her hips on his pelvis, grinding her pussy against his cock.

Pussy . . . cock . . . pussy . . . cock. Oh, God, she felt so dirty . . . and sexy.

"Oh, man, you are one hot whore," Jake exclaimed as his cock twitched against her.

She circled her arms around his neck and buried his face in her tits. The nipples, rock hard and wanting, pushed against him. He sucked on one, then the other. She gyrated, then ground hard against him . . . and received her reward. The feel of hot dampness against her panties.

He'd come in his pants. She knew he loved that—being teased to the point of no return.

"Damn, you are so fucking good at that. You like that, don't you, you little slut?"

"You know I do, baby," she murmured against his ear. "Now you're all soft, so I'd better see to your friend."

She stood up and peeled off her G-string and knelt in front of Trey. Aware of Jake watching behind her, she wrapped her fingers around Trey's cock, which curved toward his belly, and stroked up and down. She wrapped her lips around it and sucked him right down to the hilt, opening her throat wide to take him all in. She bobbed up and down on him, bringing him to the brink, but not allowing him to go over. When he seemed ready to burst despite her careful manipulation, she stood up and moved to the easy chair beside the couch. As she leaned over and grasped the back of it, she glanced over her shoulder, sending Trey an inviting smile.

Immediately, he stood up and approached her. He stood behind her and his arms circled her waist as he thrust straight into her with no preamble. Her wet, slick pussy welcomed him as he pumped into her, then groaned and came inside her. He kept thrusting and she felt an orgasm explode through her, carrying her to a delightful bliss.

She sighed as Trey pulled out, then she turned. Jake was sitting on the couch, pumping his now hard cock. She stepped toward him and crouched over him, placing one knee on either side of him, then she grasped his cock and fed it inside her. His hands grasped her waist as she slumped down on him, taking him fully inside her, then she lifted and dropped on his lap, again and again, driving his cock deep and hard into her until they both wailed in release once again.

She slid off him and slumped contentedly against his side. Trey handed her a stemmed glass of white wine and she took a sip.

A knock sounded at the door.

She glanced at Jake, then at her clothing heaped on the floor.

"I should get—"

"Don't worry about it. I'm expecting another friend."

As Trey answered the door, Harmony stood up, ready to dodge into the other room if it was room service, or some other stranger. He pulled the door open to reveal . . . Mia. Mixed emotions swirled through Harmony as she faced the woman who had caused her so much self-doubt.

Mia glanced at Harmony then her gaze snapped away, as though embarrassed by Harmony's nudity.

"I . . . uh, came to see Trey."

"Mia, come in. Join us." Trey drew her into the room.

Harmony didn't know if this was an act as part of Jake's scenario, or if the woman showing up had been a surprise.

"This is Kiki, a hooker who has been hired to entertain us," Trey told Mia.

"Come in, Mia." Jake smiled. "I'm sure you'll enjoy her talents, too."

"Well, I don't know. I don't want to intrude."

"Not at all," Harmony said, trying her best to hide the trace of resentment she felt toward the other woman. "I'm here to please Jake and whomever else he wants me to. I'm a hooker. It's what I do."

Mia's lips turned up in a small smile and Harmony could understand what Aiden saw in her. She had a pretty smile. Cute, and it made her eyes light up.

Damn, it wasn't the woman Harmony resented, but the fact that Aiden cared for her. It wasn't fair to hold it against her, and it certainly wasn't fair to ruin Jake's fantasy. This could be just the way to get over the jealousy that was putting such a strain on her and Aiden.

Harmony held out her hand to Mia. She stepped into the room and toward Harmony. Harmony leaned toward her ear.

"We're playing out Jake's fantasy tonight. I bet he'd love it if you got involved. Do you want to play along?"

"You don't mind?" she asked.

"Of course not." Raising her voice so the others could hear, she said, "These two men are spent, but I bet with a little visual stimulation they'll be raring to go again."

Harmony trailed her hand from Mia's neck to her stomach, then she pressed her hand against her chest and backed her up to the chair.

"Sit," she said.

Mia sat down. Harmony released the buttons of Mia's floral blouse, one by one, parting the fabric to show the creamy skin beneath. She pulled apart the fabric, revealing a pink lace bra, then dropped the blouse over Mia's shoulders and to the floor. She slid her hands behind Mia and released the bra, then drew it from the woman's body. The nipples on her pert, upturned breasts immediately hardened.

Aiden knocked on the door, waiting with anticipation for the door to open. He could hardly wait to see what Harmony was doing. Was she sucking Trey's cock? Jake's? Would one of the men be fucking her? Or both of them?

The door opened and Trey glanced briefly at Aiden, then his gaze darted to something going on in the room. Aiden stepped inside and followed Trey's gaze.

Oh, my God.

The sight of Mia sitting on the chair, her breasts bare, with Harmony kneeling in front of her licking her nipple, sent an immediate rush of adrenaline through his system. His cock inflated painfully in the confines of his jeans.

"Aiden." Mia glanced at him, wide-eyed, then stared at Harmony questioningly. Harmony glanced toward Aiden, her expression giving nothing away.

He licked his lips, ready to turn around and stride back through the door, but Harmony gave an almost imperceptible nod, then leaned back to Mia's chest and sucked her nipple.

Mia relaxed into the chair again and Aiden watched in

fascination as Harmony unfastened Mia's jeans and tugged them downward. Mia lifted herself so the pants could slide away, then Harmony pulled them off her ankles. Next, she peeled away the tiny pink panties.

Harmony rested a hand on each of Mia's knees and eased her legs wide open. Mia's pert little pussy glistened in the soft light. Harmony kissed up her thigh, then pressed her tongue against Mia's wet pussy and licked. Mia moaned.

Harmony's tongue pushed into the pink folds and disappeared inside Mia's slit. Mia arched and moaned. Harmony licked, then covered her clit. Aiden's cock was rock hard, as were Trey's and Jake's. The two other men stroked their members as they watched the two women. Soon Jake stood up and took Mia's hand, then drew her from the chair.

As Harmony began to stand up, Jake rested his hand on her shoulder.

"Stay there, my sexy siren," he said. "You are so fucking talented."

She stayed on her knees and watched as he gestured for Aiden to sit in the chair.

"Sit down, my friend. Enjoy."

Aiden's gaze darted to Mia then back to Harmony. He moved toward the chair and sat down.

"Do you want me to leave?" he whispered.

"Just sit down and shut up," she murmured, grinning at him.

She unfastened the button on his jeans, then pulled down his zipper.

That certainly seems to be a clear indication that I should stay.

He avoided glancing in Mia's direction, not wanting to see her pert breasts and naked pussy. Actually, wanting to see them, but not wanting to be affected by them. Because that made him want to touch her. Instead, he concentrated on Harmony's luscious naked body in front of him.

Harmony watched as Aiden dropped his pants and sat on the chair in front of her, smiling encouragement. His long, hard, familiar cock stood in front of her and she leaned forward and kissed the tip affectionately.

She probably should have accepted his offer to leave. With Mia here, things could get sticky, but Harmony didn't want to ruin the evening by making things awkward . . . and she was too caught up in the sexy, naughty fantasy to stop things now. She knew Aiden had found it exciting watching her pleasure Mia. And now she wanted to suck Aiden's cock in front of everyone . . . and wanted Aiden to see her fuck the other men . . . and to be fucked by Aiden in front of them. And in front of Mia.

She licked the length of his shaft.

"Suck his cock, baby," Jake encouraged. "Show us how hot you are."

She licked around the corona, then wrapped her lips around him and slowly lowered her mouth over him, licking and squeezing on the way down. He groaned as she swallowed him deep, then began sucking him hard between her tongue and the roof of her mouth. Squeezing and sucking, pressing on him firmly.

Someone stepped up behind her and stroked her naked bottom. Hands wrapped around her hips and drew her to her feet, while she stayed bent at the waist, sucking Aiden's cock. A cock nudged against her slick vagina, the hard head pushing its way inside her. Slowly. Deeper. Tunneling into her wet passage.

Her teeth lightly brushed Aiden's cock as her tongue swirled along the shaft. The cock behind her drove deeper. She sucked on Aiden and he groaned. Jake's cock—she could tell by how long and straight it was—pushed in to the hilt, then he drew back, dragging against her inner walls. She clutched him tight inside her as she sucked deeply on Aiden.

Jake thrust forward, then pulled back. She wanted to moan, but her mouth was full of cock. She sucked, then gave a start at the deep thrust of Jake's long cock inside her. He held tight to her hips and thrust in and out. Deep and hard. She squeezed Aiden hard, then sucked. He groaned as Jake sped up, impaling her faster and faster. She gasped in air, then began to pump Aiden's cock with the same rhythm of Jake's thrusting.

In. Out. Harder and harder.

Aiden stiffened, then jerked and hot liquid flooded her mouth. It spilled down her chin as she gasped, pleasure spiking through her at Jake's continued thrusts. He grabbed her and held her hard to his body as he spasmed inside her. She wailed, the orgasm erupting inside her in a cataclysm of pleasure.

She gasped, then flopped down on Aiden's lap. Jake pulled out of her and Aiden immediately grasped her shoulders and pressed her back, easing her onto the floor. Even though she'd just sucked him dry, he prowled over her and set his cock to her pussy, then drove in deep.

His obvious desire for her sent a thrill through her. He pounded into her, stoking the need already well fueled within her. She roared in pleasure as the orgasm overcame her, shooting her into a realm of pure ecstasy.

Aiden wanted her. Aiden loved her.

Then she heard it. A woman crying out in pleasure. She glanced over her shoulder to see Trey fucking Mia with his thick, exquisite cock on the couch. And Aiden's gaze was locked on the sight.

Damn it! It wasn't Harmony who had driven his desire to such an extraordinary level. The whole time she'd been giving him head, he'd been watching Mia!

EIGHTEEN

Cole watched Harmony as she sipped her drink. They sat in the lounge at a cozy round table by the window overlooking the view of the ocean.

"It's not a matter of trust," she said as she stared out over the glistening water. "I don't believe he's going to make love to her behind my back."

The sun had settled below the horizon, casting rich reds, blues, and purples across the sky. The water glimmered as it reflected the dark hues.

"What is bothering you then?" he asked.

"He still has feelings for her." Her fingers tensed around her frosty glass. "I think he's still in love with her."

As much as he hated the pain Harmony was experiencing, excitement streamed through him at the prospect that he might have a chance to win Harmony for himself.

"Why do you think that?"

"I told you that he asked Mia to marry him. *She* turned

him down. I can't see any reason why he wouldn't want to marry her now that she wants him back."

"But you knew all that days ago. What's happened since then?"

She stared down at her drink, swirling the straw around and around. "Last night, when he was making love to me, I realized he was watching Mia. She was with Trey behind me. That's what turned him on so much. Not me."

He leaned forward and smiled at her. "Sweetheart, I think you're underestimating how sexy you are."

Despite her heavy heart, she smiled at him. "It's not a question of self-esteem. It's clear he wants her . . . and I believe he loves her. How can I marry him knowing both those things are true?"

He brushed her hair back from her face, tucking a lock of hair behind her ear. "Do you love Aiden?"

Harmony nodded. Of course she loved him. "I don't know—" Her throat constricted, so she took a quick sip of her drink. "—what to do."

She loved Aiden, and she believed he loved her, too, but he was clearly still hung up on Mia, and Harmony knew that at some point, the adrenaline rush of being at this exotic resort in this exciting sexual situation would wane and he'd realize he didn't want a wife who acted like a slut monkey once a year. At that point, the scales would tip in Mia's favor. Even though Mia was participating, too, he could discount that as anomalous behavior on her part—unlike the twelve years

Harmony had been doing it—then they could console each other at having been caught up with this group of sexual misfits.

Aiden had sat down at the table in the lounge not realizing Harmony and Cole sat only a couple of tables away. He hadn't intended to eavesdrop, but when he'd heard Cole's question—*Do you love Aiden?*—he'd frozen.

Then Harmony's words thrust a stake through his heart.

I don't know.

What did she mean she didn't know?

Cole took Harmony's hand in his. "Sweetheart, I would never want to break up a happy couple, but you two . . ."

He kissed the back of her hand, and tingles danced up her arm.

"There's something I want to ask you. You know you and I have something special between us. We've always known that. But because of the rules we set up as a group long ago, we kept our relationship as friends . . ." His thumb stroked over her lower lip. ". . . and lovers."

He took her other hand and drew her closer.

"I think it's about time to question those rules."

She gazed at him with wide eyes, her heart thumping in her chest.

"What are you saying, Cole?"

"I'm saying that I love you . . . and the rules be damned."

He leaned forward and captured her lips in a searing, passionate kiss.

"Harmony, I love you. I want you to be with me."

Her breath caught. How many times had she dreamed of being in Cole's arms during the long months between vacations. Sometimes she'd imagined them getting married . . . sharing a life together . . . now, here she was faced with the possibility of making all those dreams a reality.

She and Cole had a closeness she had never experienced with anyone else. And he was a red-hot lover. Generous. Tender. Imaginative.

It would be so easy to say yes. To throw herself into his arms and bask in the loving moment. With Cole, she had no worries about how to behave in bed, or whether he'd accept her wild and sometimes wanton urges.

But she loved Aiden.

Deeply and truly loved him.

"Oh, Cole." She hugged him tight, trying desperately to figure out what to say. "I love you. I always have . . ."

Aiden's heart compressed and he had trouble breathing.

She loves Cole. I've lost her.

He'd never felt such pain as the burrowing ache in his heart right now.

Not even when Mia had left him.

Aiden pushed himself to his feet and strode from the lounge, hoping his legs would carry him out without stumbling.

As Harmony held Cole, she could feel their hearts thumping as one. He eased away from her, his somber gaze capturing hers. As they stared at each other, she knew he could read the answer in her eyes, just as she could see the heartbreaking disappointment in his.

She touched his cheek tenderly.

"You know, I think you love me the same way I love you . . . as very close, and very intimate friends. Neither one of us wants this relationship to end." She leaned forward and kissed him gently, then smiled at him. "And you know what? I'm not going to let it."

Aiden felt like crap. His ego lay in a puddle around his ankles. Harmony, the woman he loved . . . the woman he'd asked to marry him . . . didn't know if she loved him or not and was now considering dumping him for another guy.

A guy who clearly had a better chance with her than Aiden did.

Is that why she'd brought him along with her? To compare him to Cole before she made her decision? Maybe even to make Cole jealous so he'd pop the question?

It wasn't a bad strategy. Show Cole that someone else was interested and that he was in imminent danger of losing her forever.

It certainly would have worked on Aiden. But he had given himself so fully to Harmony she hadn't needed any tricks or subterfuge to win his heart. Now it was lost and so was she.

He'd seen her in Cole's arms. The tenderness . . . the affection.

He knocked on the door of the three-bedroom suite. It opened a moment later.

"Aiden? Nikki smiled. "Decided to join our game after all?"

He simply nodded. He desperately needed a distraction from his pain. She grabbed his hand and dragged him into the room.

"Well, great, come on in. We needed another player to even things out."

He'd heard that Trey and Mia had plans tonight, so Nikki must be with Jake and Angela. That meant they were short a guy.

He glanced around and didn't see anyone in the living room.

"Where are the others?"

She giggled. "They're in hiding. Here, put this on." She handed him a black satin blindfold. "It's part of the game."

As he placed it over his eyes and tied it behind his head, he realized it was soft fleece on the other side, which cushioned his eyes and blocked out all the light.

"Is it good and tight?" she asked. "Can you see anything?"

"Not a thing."

"Good." She took his hand and led him into the room. A moment later, she pushed lightly against his chest, backing him up. He felt something against the backs of his calves. "You can sit down. The couch is behind you.

"Okay, so this is how it works. No one knows who else is here. Except me, of course. I'll go get everyone else blindfolded, too, and then I'll draw names and pair up couples. I'll then lead each couple to a room. I'll blindfold myself, too, even though I'll know who I'm with. Then we'll go to it." She giggled again. "Feel our way around, you know?"

In the pitch blackness, he began to think about Harmony and his pain, but he pushed the thoughts aside and concentrated on the sounds in the apartment. He heard voices and giggles in the other rooms, and feet padding across floors. Soon, he heard clothing being cast aside and soft moans. He paid attention to the sounds, listening, not wanting his thoughts to drift back to—

He heard someone walk into the room. "I'm going to leave you two here," Nikki said. "I'm not going to say anything, so for all you know I might be here watching." She giggled.

After a moment, he felt a hand touch his chest, then pat down his stomach to his belt. He could feel the warmth of her body as she knelt down in front of him and rested her other hand on his knee. He opened his legs and she moved between them. Her hand fumbled with his belt, then released it. She drew down the zipper of his pants and her soft hand reached inside and wrapped around his shaft.

It was probably Nikki, her comment that she might stay and watch being a lame, but cute, way of trying to throw him off.

Her soft lips pressed against the tip of him in a warm kiss, then her lips parted and encircled his cock-head in her hot, wet mouth. Her tongue swirled over him and he almost groaned, but subdued it, increasing his excitement.

She teased and cajoled him, her tongue twirling around his cock, gliding over the ultra-sensitive skin under the corona. He swelled inside her mouth as her tongue and lips glided down his shaft. She sucked and he arched farther into her mouth. Her hands cupped his balls and gently massaged them. He felt the heat build, then his body tensed as he came closer and closer. She sucked again and he erupted into her mouth, pulsing and pulsing as she swallowed.

He slumped back on the couch and she curled up beside him. He rested his hand on her thigh, then slid upward until he found her hips, then slid his hand under her top. As his hand glided over her breast, still encased in a bra, he felt her squirming as she released fastenings and slid off her top. A moment later, fabric slid across his legs as she removed her pants. She took his other hand and pressed something into it. Silk panties is what it felt like. A second later, the bra tugged from under his hand and now he grasped a smooth, silky mound. The nipple hardened, pressing into his palm.

He pushed himself forward and knelt down, then turned

toward her. He shifted between her legs and leaned forward until he felt the soft skin of her stomach on his cheek. He kissed upward until his lips came into contact with the bottom of her breast. He stroked it with his hand and toyed with the nipple, teasing it between his finger and thumb. She sighed.

He shifted upward and licked the tip of the nipple, then drew it into his mouth. She drew in a breath as he sucked, then twirled his tongue around the aureole. He slid his mouth away and stroked with his finger as he slid sideways to grasp the other nipple in his mouth. After bringing both nipples to incredible hardness, he kissed downward to her soft, wet slit. His tongue found her clit and she clutched his head with both hands as he licked and sucked the tiny button. He slipped his thumb inside her, then curled his finger around to slip into her back entrance, then he squeezed as he continued to suck on her clit.

She tightened her grip on his head and arched forward. She gasped, then wailed in release as an orgasm shuddered through her body.

His wilted cock swelled to life as she pushed him backward onto the floor. She climbed over him and her hand grasped his cock and held it upright, then he felt her cleft glide over him, then swallow him inside.

She leaned forward and her lips locked with his, her tongue licking his lips then sliding inside his mouth.

Oh, God, it was Mia. He knew it. In fact, he realized he'd known it on some level from the moment she'd touched him.

By the smell of her skin. By the taste of her. By the way his fingers fit inside her. And now his cock was buried deep in her core.

He should pull out. Stop this right now. He'd promised Harmony.

But he couldn't. He needed Mia right now. Her warmth. Her touch. The way she made him feel loved.

And what did his promise to Harmony matter now?

Mia loved him, and he needed to feel that right now.

He drove deep into her. She wrapped her arms around him and moved with him, squeezing him with her internal muscles. She knew who he was, too, he was sure of it.

She moved up and down on him, driving him deeper into her body. The feel of her warm, silky channel caressing him with every thrust drove him wild. She tightened around him and he felt the pleasure build. She sucked in a breath and moaned.

"Oh, my God. Aiden."

Harmony's voice. From across the room.

But he couldn't stop. Mia drove up and down on him, taking him deep . . . again and again. She wailed in orgasm as he erupted inside her, the pleasure sweeping through him in a carnal release of primal bliss.

Gasping for air, Mia dropped to his chest, snuggling against him. He slipped his finger under the blindfold and tugged it aside. Mia's soft, auburn hair swirled across his face, the familiar delicate scent of organic shampoo tickling his senses. He shifted his gaze sideways and saw Harmony staring down at him from the doorway, her features twisted in an expression of horror.

Gently, he grasped Mia's shoulders and eased her to a sitting position. She glanced at Aiden, no surprise on her face—so she'd known, too—then her gaze shifted to Harmony and darted away, a guilty expression on her face. She gathered her clothing and stood up.

"I'll leave you two alone," Mia said and headed toward the kitchen.

"Aiden . . ."

Aiden stood up and tugged on his pants as the silence hung around them. He sat down on the couch, his folded hands hanging between his knees.

Harmony shook her head. "The blindfolds . . . Tell me you didn't know it was Mia."

He was tempted. It would be so easy. But what did it matter? Harmony had already decided against him.

"I won't lie to you, Harmony. I knew it was Mia."

NINETEEN

Aiden watched Harmony race out the door, pain etching her features.

Mia stepped through the kitchen doorway and sat down beside him. She took his hand.

"I'm sorry, Aiden."

He glanced toward her. Mia. His Mia. The woman he had longed for ever since she'd left him almost two years ago. Now that he knew Harmony didn't want him anymore, he realized he was free to renew his relationship with Mia. He could finally have the future with this woman that he'd dreamed about so often.

As he gazed at her face, he realized . . . that's not what he wanted. When he'd lost her, he'd felt so devastated. But nothing like what he felt now, losing Harmony.

Whatever love he'd felt for Mia was gone. Or had never been. Now that he loved Harmony—and her wanting to be with another man didn't change that—he realized she was the only woman he loved. Or had ever truly loved.

He had shared something special with Mia, but it wasn't real love. In fact, he now realized that the lingering feelings he had for her were simply feelings for someone he cared about. He would always care about Mia, and be protective toward her. That's the kind of relationship they'd had.

That's probably why she'd run away from his proposal. Deep inside, she must have recognized it, too. She must have realized on some level that she was using him as a crutch.

The fact that she'd come here to renew their relationship was simply because she'd found herself alone, and Mia didn't like to be alone.

"Mia, you came here because you said you wanted to pick up where we left off . . ."

She drew her hand from his and shook her head. "I'm sorry, Aiden. It won't work."

"Are you turning me down again?" he asked.

She looked stricken as she stared at him.

"When I came here to try and win you back, I thought I had it all figured out." She laughed in spite of herself. "But now I realize that I was just scared to be alone. You'd always made me feel secure. I think I mistook that security for love. I'm so sorry, Aiden, but I just don't love you the way you deserve to be loved."

Aiden chuckled. "It's okay. I was just going to say that I think you made the right choice when you left me. We were both looking for something and we thought we'd found it in each other but . . ." He shrugged. "We were wrong."

She nodded. "Do you think you'll be able to patch it up with Harmony?"

He shook his head. "She's in love with someone else."

"Cole?"

So she'd seen it, too. She rested her hand on his arm.

"I'm so sorry, Aiden. You deserve better."

His heart ached at the thought that he'd lost Harmony. He sucked in a breath and took Mia's hand.

"What about you? Have you hooked up with Trey?"

It had been clear she had a special attraction to the man.

Her cheeks flushed pink. "He's great. I really like him."

"Are you going to keep seeing him—afterward?"

He didn't know where the man lived, but if they were serious about each other, they could make a relationship work.

"No."

"No?"

"I like him . . . a lot . . . but it's enough that we have this time together. For so long, my sense of self-worth has been totally linked to whatever man I had in my life. And if I didn't have a man in my life, I felt worthless. Being with these people this week . . . being so totally accepted, with no expectations . . . has made me feel better about myself. And seeing how much it's possible to enjoy myself without a boyfriend, makes me want to get to know myself for a while . . . find out who I am alone before I hook up with another man. When I'm ready, then I can find out who I am as part of a couple."

"Good for you." He squeezed her hand, then frowned. "It looks like I'll have to learn how to find happiness alone, too."

Harmony locked the door between her room and Aiden's, then threw herself onto the bed in tears.

How could he have . . . ? He'd made love to Mia after promising he wouldn't. He loved Mia, he wanted *her*.

The pain seeped through every part of her. She'd lost him. Tears flowed with a new vigor and she sobbed into her pillow.

Sometime later, Harmony heard a soft knocking on the adjoining door. She froze, worried Aiden would come in—she couldn't handle seeing him right now—then she remembered she'd locked the door. Another knock.

Then silence.

Once she was sure he'd given up, she tugged the damp pillow from under her head and tossed it to the floor, then snuggled against the one on the other side of the bed. Now, she lay there, wishing for the oblivion of sleep, but it eluded her.

She ached knowing Aiden lay in the next room. She could just open the door between their two rooms and climb into his bed . . . and into his arms. She longed to feel his body close to hers, to feel his hand stroke her hair in that comforting way he had, especially when she was feeling down. Somehow, in the midst of her tears and heartache, she dozed off with that comforting image in her mind.

The next morning, sunlight washed across her face and she opened her eyes to a new day. She had lost Aiden. But did it have to be that way?

He still loved Mia, he still wanted her, but that didn't mean he wanted her more than he wanted Harmony. She hadn't even given him a chance to choose between them. She'd told him she loved him, but when he'd asked her to marry him, she hadn't answered him. He didn't know what her answer would have been.

Ever since his proposal, he had to have been feeling rejected by her—then along came Mia, his previous love. How could Harmony really blame him for falling prey to the temptation of a woman who was more than willing to marry him?

That didn't mean he wanted Mia over Harmony. If she gave him a chance to discuss it with her . . .

Damn it, she'd been running on fear. Because of her own insecurities, she hadn't given him the answer burning in her heart.

She had been afraid Aiden would not accept her for who she was, that he would see her in this environment and reject her. Even after he'd shown time and time again that he not only made no negative judgment about her behavior, but applauded her with enthusiasm . . . she still worried that he would eventually "come to his senses" and see her for the tramp she was. At least, the tramp she believed herself to be. But that was based on other people's judgments of her. Like that jerk Lance. She had to take back her self-esteem. Believe in herself. And even put herself in a situation where she might be rejected.

Because losing Aiden was not an option she would accept easily.

Aiden stepped from his shower and dressed, then knocked on Harmony's door again. She didn't answer. He tried the knob, but this time, unlike last night, it was unlocked.

He opened the door and peered into the room. No sign of Harmony. He stepped inside and checked the bathroom. The door was open and the small room was empty.

He went down to the restaurant on the terrace, her favorite place for breakfast, but he couldn't find her. He ran across Trey by the pool but he hadn't seen her. Aiden searched the resort, determined to find her and try to convince her he loved *her,* not Mia. He wanted to win her back. If only she would give him a chance.

After two hours, he finally gave up looking and returned to the lobby. He pressed the elevator call button and waited.

She'd have to return to the room eventually. He'd go up and plunk down in her room and wait her out.

Once he got to her door, he pulled out the VIP card he

had—the one each of the group members had that gave them special access, including the rooms of each of the other group members.

He walked into her room and realized she'd been here. Her purse sat on the dresser and her favorite sandals lay askew inside the open cupboard, as though she'd carelessly kicked them off. Maybe she'd gone down to the pool. Typically, she took her straw beach bag and wore her flip-flops when she went out to go swimming.

He plunked down in one of the armchairs and turned on the television. On the screen, a meteor flew across the sky and smashed into a building. People screamed and cars crashed. Another meteor crushed a truck. Aiden settled back to watch.

"Aiden?" The adjoining door opened. "Are you in there?" Harmony stepped through the door.

Aiden flicked the television off and sat up straight.

"Harmony."

She didn't look angry, but her mouth looked grim. She was definitely tense.

"Aiden, I need to talk to you."

His jaw clenched. *Here it comes. The breakup.*

She stepped farther into the room and stood in front of him.

"Aiden, I know you love Mia . . ."

"Harmony, Mia and I—"

"Please." She blinked, her eyes shimmering. "Let me say what I need to say."

She dropped to one knee in front of him, her hand resting on his thigh.

His cock lurched while his stomach tightened.

An insane thought dashed through his head. Was she going to give him a blowjob? Now?

The thought of her full lips gliding around his growing cock made his heartbeat accelerate. *It's always a good time for a blowjob,* a lustful voice sang inside his head, but he ignored it as best he could.

"Harmony, what are you doing?"

Maybe she intended to give him one last tumble before she dumped him.

She gazed into his eyes and her hand moved, but she grasped his hand, not his cock.

"I have something I want to say to you."

Oh, God, here it comes. He steeled himself.

"I want to . . ." She cleared her throat. "I mean, will you . . . ?"

She sucked in a deep breath and stammered, "Good heavens, how do you men do this? I never thought it would be so hard."

"Just spit it out, Harmony. You just want to . . . ?" he prompted.

She nodded and cleared her throat again. She took his hand in both of hers and met his gaze. She blinked, then drew in a deep breath.

"Aiden, I love you with all my heart. Will you marry me?"

"What? Did you just—did I hear you right?"

"I was an idiot to hesitate when you asked me. I was afraid you wouldn't accept the real me but I finally realized that it was me who wasn't accepting the real Harmony. I've decided I like who I am." She gripped his hand tighter. "You have been totally accepting of who I am. I should never have worried about that. I know you care about Mia, but . . . I'm hoping I still have a chance."

"Harmony." He pulled her into his arms and kissed her. "Of course I'll marry you."

She eased back and stared at him with wide eyes. "You will?"

He chuckled. "Don't look so surprised. I did ask you to marry me in the first place."

"I know but . . . now that Mia is available."

"Harmony, I never loved Mia. I just loved how she made me feel needed. You, on the other hand, make me feel loved."

He kissed her again. When their lips parted, she drew back.

"I also want to make clear that . . . I intend to keep coming to these vacations with my friends. They are very important to me . . ." She straightened her back and held her head high. "And it's part of who I am."

He dragged her against his body and held her tight.

"I wouldn't have it any other way." He stroked her head. "So I guess this means you won't be marrying Cole."

"You knew about that?"

"I was in the lounge when you were talking. I didn't mean to overhear."

"But you must not have heard the whole thing."

"I heard you say you love him. That you've always loved him."

"And I do. As a friend. We were both a little confused about that for a while, but when he asked me to marry him, I realized it's you I love." She smiled and stroked his cheek. "Just you."

EPILOGUE

Harmony gazed at herself in the full-length mirror, tucking an errant lock of hair into place in her elegant updo. She wore a white satin brocade corset with delicate lace trim. The underwire cups held her breasts high and the sweetheart neckline revealed the swell of her soft flesh.

She sat down and pulled on a stocking, then drew it up her leg and fastened it to the garters attached to the garter belt she wore under the corset with tiny satin bows. Once she'd finished pulling on and attaching the second stocking, she returned to the dresser and pulled on the long white satin gloves sitting there, then she stepped into her white satin shoes with narrow five-inch heels. She glanced in the mirror again.

Oh, she'd almost forgotten. She couldn't go to her wedding without . . .

She walked to the bed and picked up the white lace headpiece with gathered tulle flowing from it. She settled the headpiece over her dark hair, then pushed hairpins in to keep it in place.

She turned around then peered over her shoulder to see the reflection of her back in the mirror. Through the soft haze of the tulle veil, she could see her bare buttocks, set off by the small triangle of white lace at the top, the only part of her thong visible from the back.

Ready. She picked up the bouquet of white silk roses, then walked to the door and peered out. Nikki nodded and started the music, a CD playing from the entertainment center in the condo, then returned to her chair. The wedding march began and Harmony stepped into the hallway. As she entered the living room, the guests—Nikki, Angela, Trey, Jake, and Mia—all fully dressed in semiformal wear, turned to watch her walk through the room toward the eating counter where Aiden stood waiting for her, dressed in a pair of briefs that looked like a tuxedo. Cole stood beside him, wearing a black T-shirt and briefs. He was presiding over their mock wedding.

They'd have the official wedding after they returned home, the one with family and work friends and all, but to Harmony, this was the real wedding, the one with her closest and most intimate friends.

Aiden beamed at her the whole time she walked down the short aisle formed by having moved the chairs and couch aside. When she reached his side, he took her hand and they turned toward Cole, their backs to their gathered friends.

Harmony was intensely aware of everyone's gaze on her. It felt extremely naughty to be dressed all in white, yet have her bare behind framed by the white corset, thong, and stockings.

"Dear friends, we are gathered here to witness the joining of Harmony and Aiden," Cole began.

Harmony glanced at Aiden and smiled. She couldn't wait for the end of the ceremony so she could physically join with him—which wouldn't be long because they had purposely chosen to keep the speaking part short.

"I have known and loved Harmony for a long time," Cole continued, "just as every one of you has, and I know we all wish her well in her new life with Aiden. Would the two of you face each other and join both hands?"

Harmony turned to face Aiden and he reached for her other hand and grasped it in the warmth of his. She couldn't stop smiling at him.

"Now you may share your vows."

Aiden drew her right hand to his mouth and kissed it tenderly.

"Harmony, I love you as I have no other. I will cherish you in my life always and I will encourage you to embrace life and love in any way you so chose. Together I know we will find a happiness that will make us complete, and I look forward to sharing that happiness with the friends gathered here today—at least once a year."

"Aiden, I love you from the depths of my soul and I want

to share my life with you, including new and exciting experiences. I also want to share my friends with you, along with our most erotic sexual fantasies."

There were no rings to exchange, or papers to sign. That would all be part of the official wedding. Short and sweet is what they'd wanted today, then a chance to celebrate with their friends.

"I pronounce you husband and wife," Cole stated. "You may kiss the bride."

Aiden took Harmony into his arms and kissed her thoroughly and with passion. Once their lips parted, Cole grinned at her.

"Now it's my turn to kiss the bride."

Aiden released her hands and Harmony turned to face Cole. He wrapped his arms around her and kissed her soundly, his tongue slipping into her mouth and swirling around. His hands found her bare buttocks and he cupped them and pulled her tight against his pelvis. She could feel his bulge pressed against her. It was wonderfully hard and she ached for that long, hard shaft to slide inside her.

Cole released her and Aiden drew her back into his arms and kissed her deeply, his tongue moving inside her mouth where Cole's had just been. Aiden's hard cock pushed against her while Cole's hands roamed over her butt. Aiden's fingers found the hooks on the back of her corset and he began unfastening them. Slowly, the tight garment released, first from around her ribs, then her stomach, and finally from her hips. Aiden peeled the corset away. Cole slid his fingers under the delicate lace of her thong and found the snap on one side, then flipped it open while Aiden found the snap on the other side. Aiden tugged on the scrap of lace. It slid forward, between her legs, dragging over her sensitive flesh. Once it was free of her body, he crumpled it in his hand, then tossed it to the waiting crowd. Jake snatched it from the air and smiled, then pushed it into the pocket of his suit jacket.

Now she stood in front of everyone, her torso totally naked, except for the brief, white lace garter belt. Everything of importance was totally exposed, but she still wore long white gloves, white high heels, and her veil—which made her feel even more naked. Moisture pooled inside her.

"I think the groom should do more than kiss the bride," Jake called out.

Harmony slid her hand over the bulge in Aiden's briefs, then slid her hand inside and grasped his big, hard cock. She pulled him free, then crouched in front of him and wrapped her lips around his cock-head. It was big and hard and filled her mouth so full. She sucked on him. His shaft swelled even more within the grasp of her hand. She swallowed him deeper, continuing to suck on him. Cole crouched down behind Harmony and cupped her breasts as her head bobbed up and down on Aiden. He groaned as she cupped his balls and pleasured his shaft, while Cole tweaked her nipples, sending sparks of need firing through her.

She smiled up at Aiden, then turned to face Cole. He drew his cock from his boxers and she wrapped her hand around him and licked around the corona, then drew him into her mouth. Aiden stroked her ass, around and around, making her hotter and needier as she glided up and down on Cole's erection. Aiden's fingertips brushed against her moist opening and she sucked in a breath.

Cole stroked her hair as she sucked him deeper. Aiden brushed her again, then his fingertip probed more firmly over her hot, wet flesh.

The feel of Cole's big cock filling her mouth, then Aiden's finger slipping inside her from behind, nearly sent her into orgasm. She swirled her tongue over Cole, then sucked him hard, squeezing him inside her mouth. Aiden pushed another finger into her and she moaned against Cole's cock. Aiden's fingers thrust a few times, then they slipped out and grazed over her clit. She was overtaken by a light, easy climax that she knew was only the beginning.

She stood up and the two men closed in around her. Cole pressed against the front of her and Aiden against the back of her. Cole kissed her, his tongue cajoling hers lightly, then he turned her around to face Aiden. Aiden claimed her lips, urgently kissing her and stroking her lips with his tongue. A moment later, Cole's cock pressed against her buttocks.

Cole prodded gently at her ass as Aiden leaned down to suck her breast. Cole's cock-head eased into her, slowly stretching her. Aiden cupped his hands on her buttocks and pulled her tight to him, at the same time separating her cheeks to give Cole easier access. The pressure built as his cock-head penetrated her while Aiden kissed her. Cole pushed in deeper, his shaft sliding into her. She felt so full with his cock fully inside her.

Aiden's cock nudged her front opening and his cock-head slipped inside. He pushed forward until she was fully impaled on his cock, too. The three of them stood there, Harmony sandwiched tight between these two special men, their cocks filling her. Then Aiden began to move. His gentle thrusts pushed her harder into the crook of Cole's body, pushing his cock deeper into her ass. Aiden thrust, then thrust again. Deeper and harder.

Double pleasure shot through her with shattering intensity. She moaned as the two cocks glided into her in unison, driving deep and hard, filling her with intense pleasure.

Cole cupped her breasts. Aiden's finger trailed down her stomach then into her slit. He found her clit and stroked it. Intense pleasure spiked through her and she exploded in orgasm. Her wail, long and loud, filled the room as she rode the ecstatic wave of bliss. Cole and Aiden groaned at the same time. The feel of hot liquid filling her pussy and her ass triggered another orgasm. She moaned and clung to Aiden as the two men continued to thrust into her.

Ecstasy thrummed through every part of her, consuming her. Slowly, it faded, leaving an echo of bliss pulsating through her body as she gasped for breath.

"That was absolutely incredible." She sighed happily.

Aiden smiled at her then kissed her tenderly.

"You haven't forgotten about us, have you?" Jake asked.

Aiden chuckled and withdrew from Harmony's pussy. Cole eased free, also. Jake freed his cock and slipped it into Harmony's pussy. He kissed her passionately then began to thrust. In and out. Deep and hard.

As her pleasure soared, she realized that beside her, Aiden was fucking Nikki. Jake's cock stroked Harmony's inner walls with unrelenting determination until she gasped and moaned in release. He withdrew, smiling. He kissed her and moved away. Trey stepped in front of her as Aiden finished with Nikki. Angela stood behind her. It was like a lineup.

As Trey drew her into his arms and nudged his cock against her, she realized it *was* a line . . . a receiving line. Angela stroked Aiden's cock, quickly reviving it. Trey stroked Harmony's breast, then pushed his cock inside her. Angela pulled Aiden's cock to her opening and it slid inside her. Trey moved, pistoning Harmony with his beautifully curved, steel-hard cock. Angela began to moan beside them and as Harmony watched her friend's face contort in pleasure, she felt yet another orgasm claim her.

"Congratulations, Harmony. I know you and Aiden will be very happy together." Trey gave her a great big kiss before he moved away.

Harmony turned toward the chairs and realized that Mia sat by herself, still fully dressed and clutching her knees.

Cole walked toward her, then knelt in front of her and stroked her thigh. She smiled as his hand glided upward, disappearing under the hem of her dress. She opened her legs and her head fell back against the chair. The tops of her stockings and black lacy garters showed as Cole pushed her hem higher.

Aiden's arms swept around Harmony and under her knees and he lifted her off her feet. His lips captured hers as he carried her across the room, then sat on a sturdy dining room chair, still kissing her. She drew back and stared into his warm cinnamon eyes, feeling cherished in the comfort of his arms.

He smiled, setting his brown eyes glowing. "Hello, Mrs. Curtis."

She smiled. "Hello, Mr. Curtis."

He captured her lips again. His cock swelled between their bodies. She drew herself upright and shifted around until she sat squarely on his lap facing the room. He grasped her hips and lifted, then positioned his cock against her hot slit. She lowered herself down, capturing his cock inside her, then squeezed him.

He groaned. "Honey, I'll never get tired of feeling you do that."

His hands cupped her breasts and they sat for a moment and watched the scene around them. Jake thrust into Angie from behind as she stood leaning against the back of the couch. He also stroked Trey's balls while Nikki, on her knees in front of Trey, bobbed her head up and down his hard cock. Angie watched Cole and Mia, who were both naked on the couch, Cole's cock buried in Mia's mouth.

Aiden stroked Harmony's breasts. Her bead-hard nipples pressed into his palms.

"Harmony, thank you for inviting me on this vacation with you and for sharing this side of your life with me."

He rocked his pelvis, gliding his cock into her in a rhythmic pulse. Gentle waves of pleasure swelled through her.

Across the room, Trey drew his cock from Nikki's mouth and moved to Mia. She moaned against Cole's cock as Trey knelt behind her and pressed his cock to her opening and thrust inside. Angie wailed in climax. Jake groaned and leaned against Angie, his arms wrapped around her waist, holding her close to his body. Nikki stroked Jake's ass with one hand as her other pulsed between her legs. Trey caught her arm and drew her nearer, then captured her breast in his mouth as he continued to thrust into Mia.

Cole glanced at Harmony and Aiden and smiled. He slid his cock from Mia's mouth and stood up. His hard shaft bobbed up and down as he walked toward them.

"Room for one more?" he asked.

Aiden lifted Harmony and drew his cock from her wet canal, then pressed it to her back opening. He eased her back down and his bulbous cock-head stretched her as his long shaft filled her ass. Cole crouched in front of her and pressed his purple, veined cock against her slit. He thrust forward and she gasped.

Both men filled her and exquisite pleasure built within her as they pulsed and thrust into her. Aiden, her husband, and Cole, her dearest friend. Both bringing her to climax.

She clutched at Aiden's thigh with one hand and Cole's

shoulder with the other as a powerful jolt of pleasure erupted through her, exploding into blissful, ecstatic joy.

As she slumped back against Aiden's strong chest, his arms enveloping her, Cole drew out and kissed her.

"You're a lucky man, Aiden."

Aiden's arms tightened around Harmony.

"You got that right."

Cole returned to the others and stepped behind Nikki. She turned to him and grinned, then they kissed.

Harmony glanced over her shoulder.

"I love you, Aiden."

He captured her lips in a sweet kiss.

"And I love you."

He held her close and they watched their friends pleasuring each other. Before meeting Aiden, she never would have believed that her two worlds could blend together so well. She snuggled into his arms, pleased that she would never have to hide who she was again.

READ ON FOR A PREVIEW OF OPAL CAREW'S
UPCOMING EROTIC ROMANCE

SECRET TIES

*Available from St. Martin's Griffin
in Summer 2009*

When Summer meets Max Delaney, she instantly falls under his spell. Max is a master of bondage and submission, and Summer yearns to be dominated by him body and soul. Max tutors her in the pleasures of submissive sex, and together they explore Summer's deepest, darkest fantasies. But can she surrender to her ultimate desire: to share herself with three men at once? Find out in *Secret Ties* . . .

Summer stared at the row of penises laid out in front of her—seven inches tall, standing straight up, and made of chocolate. Some dark chocolate, some milk chocolate, a couple of white chocolate, and one where she'd experimented and created a pale flesh tone made from a combination of white and milk chocolate with a dab of red.

Several people streamed by the table, some glancing at the erotic chocolates she had neatly arranged on the table, but most heading straight to the stack of books to Summer's right. Tanya's books. Summer glanced at Tanya, her friend the erotic-romance author. Tanya smiled and closed the book she'd just finished signing, then handed it to the eager couple standing in front of her.

"I loved your last book," the young woman said. "I hope this one is just as sexy."

Tanya grinned, with a glint in her eye. "If anything, it's even sexier. I don't think you'll be disappointed."

Tanya wasn't kidding. Summer had read it, red-cheeked through the whole thing, but totally engrossed. She'd never read a book about submission and bondage before, and she'd had no idea her friend knew so much about it, but then Tanya had always been full of surprises.

She glanced at the scintillating cover of Tanya's latest book, showing a leather-clad man with tight abs and a muscular chest. The hero of the book—well, the main one—was very well endowed. Summer had had more than a few intensely sexy dreams with him as the star since reading this particular book.

She glanced at Tanya, signing another book. She wondered about the type of life Tanya lived now. Did she go off with multiple men and actually experience the threesomes and moresomes she detailed in her stories? Summer couldn't imagine doing that but admired Tanya for having the guts to do it, or even just to write about it. Summer had read in the acknowledgments that a particular man, whom she referred to simply as M, had helped her with her research. Just how in-depth had that research been?

Tanya closed the book and handed it to the woman in front of her. The woman smiled broadly and clutched the book to her chest, then grasped her husband's hand and led him away, further into the *den of iniquity,* as Shane had teasingly called it when he knew Summer was going to Chicago, two hours from her home in Port Smith, to attend this trade show dedicated to adult entertainment.

She glanced around the dimly lit convention hall at the

neat rows of booths lining the aisle ways—booths with brightly colored, penis-shaped vibrators, glass dildos, skimpy lingerie, leather boots, feathers, ropes . . . and, of course, the booth she shared with Tanya with erotic chocolate and stacks of erotic-romance books. But it sure was a long way from her little chocolate shop in an upscale hotel in a small town.

Summer adjusted the chocolate suckers in front of her—cocksuckers, which were small chocolate penises on a stick—into neat rows, then shifted her attention to the stacks of Tanya's books and straightened them into neat piles. The people gathered around her booth were no longer looking at the goods on the tables. They were watching the stage and the two women on it.

One was the flamboyant Mistress of Ceremonies, who wore a slinky, low-cut red velvet dress, with a feather boa coiled around her neck. The other woman wore, well, nothing really. She did have a G-string, maybe, but mostly a few leather straps and links of metal draped around her rib cage from a harness over her shoulders. They did nothing to hide her small but pert breasts. She also wore a bridle on her head with a brightly colored feather on top. She held her arms bent forward in front of her.

The MC had a small riding crop, and she commanded the feathered woman to prance around the stage with light slaps across her behind. Summer dragged her gaze from the stage and glanced around at the people watching with interest.

She felt a prickle down the back of her neck and glanced up to see a tall, devastatingly handsome man staring at her.

He had dark eyes and black hair, cropped short and spiky. His square jaw, shadowed lightly, framed full lips, and a diamond glittered in one earlobe, making her think of a pirate prince. Her gaze jerked away, resting on the chocolates in front of her, only to realize she was staring at a life-sized chocolate erection. She glanced back to the man to find him grinning at her, as if saying *it doesn't measure up to mine*. The very thought made her flush.

He smiled at her, his eyes twinkling. She just gaped at him, totally blown away by his astounding, raw male magnetism. His dark eyes held her mesmerized, until the focus of those eyes strayed down her body, lingering on her breasts—setting a fire within her that threatened to blaze out of control—then continued past her hips. The rest of her was hidden from sight by the table, but her nipples hardened at his frank male interest, and she felt her insides melt, liquid heat gathering between her legs. She allowed her gaze to stray past his muscular shoulders to his broad chest, down to his narrow waist, then flicker over the front of his pants, wondering at the size of the male member he was hiding in those black jeans.

Good heavens, that wasn't like her. She glanced back to his face. To her horror, he smiled knowingly and her cheeks flushed in embarrassment.

He stepped toward the table and her breath caught. Was he going to talk to her? Maybe proposition her as several men had Tanya already? What would she possibly say to him?

Tanya glanced his way, and her lips turned up in a huge smile.

"Max."

The gorgeous hunk took Tanya's hand and kissed it. A pang of jealousy lanced through Summer. Which was *insane*.

"I see your book is doing well," he said.

The women in the line waiting to meet Tanya watched Max with wide eyes. He could have passed for a cover model.

Tanya winked. "Thanks to you."

Max? Was he M from the acknowledgments?

Her gaze shifted to his crotch, which had seemed to have become an obsession with her, and after a lingering gaze, shifted away again and locked onto his dark eyes, glittering with amusement.

"So who's your friend?" Max asked.

Thrilling erotic romances from
OPAL CAREW...

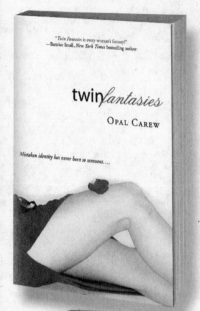

TWIN FANTASIES
Two men are better than one....

BLUSH
For every woman curious about the ancient sensual arts of Kama Sutra...

SWING
This resort is no ordinary vacation spot....